BLOOM AFTER SHAHADA

A Revert's Guide to Flourishing in Islam

Joyful Hijabi

DEDICATION

To the beloved of Allah, The seal of the Prophets, The gentle light who walked among us, **Prophet Muhammad ﷺ.**

You taught us that strength is found in stillness, That mercy is greater than anger, And that even the most broken hearts can bloom again.

You wept for us before we were born. You prayed for those who would never meet you. You called us your *brothers and sisters —* those who believed without seeing.

"There has certainly come to you a Messenger from among yourselves. Grievous to him is what you suffer; [he is] concerned over you and to the believers is kind and merciful." — Surah At-Tawbah (9:128)

You said:

"Among the most beloved of people to me are those who will come after me, and believe in me, even though they never saw me." — Musnad Ahmad

Ya Rasūl Allāh ﷺ,, This book is a whisper of love, a return, a reflection — Because your path showed me the way back to my Lord.

May peace and blessings forever be upon you.

— Joyful Hijabi

Table of Contents

Part V: Trusting the Journey-Tawakkul, Gratitude, and Hope

INTRODUCTION

From Shahada to Spiritual Spring: Why Blooming Matters

I still remember the excitement.

Not long after I embraced Islam, I made a trip to Devon Avenue in Chicago — a street full of halal restaurants, Muslim shops, and bookstores. I was a new Muslim, full of curiosity and wonder. I stepped into one of those bookstores like someone stepping into a secret garden, eager to gather whatever knowledge I could.

I didn't know what to look for exactly, but I wanted to feel equipped — and close to Allah.

So, I reached for what seemed essential: a thick Qur'an with English transliteration, a copy of Sahih al-Bukhari, and the massive Riyadh as-Salihin. Books that, in hindsight, were far too advanced to start with. But I held them like treasures. Heavy, sacred, mysterious. I wanted to understand everything — right away. I wanted to be a "good Muslim." I wanted to bloom.

But I'll be honest — I was overwhelmed.

I didn't get the chance to read them page by page like I had imagined. The books sat beautifully on my shelf, almost like sacred ornaments — reminders of my desire to grow, even if I didn't know how just yet.

No one tells you that blooming takes time.

That you don't have to start with heavyweight books to be a faithful believer.

That you'll stumble. That you'll grow in seasons. That Islam isn't something you conquer — it's something you live, inhale, and keep returning to.

I've had to unlearn a lot over the years.

I've had to soften, slow down, and remember that growth in Islam isn't always loud or visible. Sometimes it's quiet. Sometimes it happens when no one claps for you.

Sometimes blooming is just showing up for Fajr after missing it for a week. Or smiling through a hard day and whispering Alhamdulillah anyway.

This book — Bloom After Shahada — is for that stage of the journey.

It's for the new Muslim who has already embraced the truth, already tasted the roots of faith — and is now wondering, How do I thrive in this?

It's not about perfect routines or encyclopedic knowledge.

It's about joy. Confidence. Self-compassion. Healing. Presence.

It's about spiritual springtime after seasons of striving.

This is the third and final part of a series that began with Stillness After Shahada — for those first moments of shock, grief, and grounding. Then came Roots After Shahada — a deeper dive into identity, healing, and anchoring your new life in Allah.

And now: it's time to bloom.

Wherever you are in your journey — whether you took your shahada twenty days ago or twenty years ago — this book is here to remind you:

You are still growing.

You are still guided.

You are still worthy of joy.

Let's begin again — with gentleness, with light, and with a heart ready to bloom.

PART I
HEALING AFTER HARDSHIP

CHAPTER 1

THE PERMISSION TO BLOOM — EVEN AFTER PAIN

You may not feel ready to bloom.

You might still be nursing invisible wounds.

You might be holding your breath from the last storm.

You might be wondering, "Do I even deserve to grow?"

But here's the truth that faith gently whispers:

Allah doesn't wait for you to be unbroken to begin your blooming.

Sometimes we hold ourselves back because we think pain disqualifies us from joy. That healing must be "complete" before we can reach forward. That our past must be perfect before we can have permission to live freely as a Muslim with light and confidence.

But the Qur'an shows us something else entirely.

Broken Soil, Blossoming Seeds

Allah says in Surah Al-Hadid:

"Know that this worldly life is no more than play, amusement, luxury, mutual boasting, and competition in wealth and children. It is like rain that causes plants to grow, pleasing the farmers. But soon it withers, turning yellow, then becomes debris…"

(Surah Al- Hadid 57:20)

Why does Allah compare life to blooming things? Because even what flourishes eventually fades — and even what is dry can come back to life.

The soil that produces flowers was once dry. It cracked. It withstood harsh heat. It carried buried things.

But it still bloomed.

If You've Been Hurt in the Name of Religion

Many reverts carry deep emotional scars — not just from their past life, but from inside the ummah too.

You may have been shamed for not knowing everything.

You may have been judged for your clothes, your friends, your pace.

You may have been made to feel like you're too much or not enough — sometimes at the same time.

But let me say this clearly, from one revert heart to another:

You do not need to earn the right to belong. You already do.

Islam is from Allah — and His mercy outweighs any person's opinion.

Give yourself the same compassion Allah gives you.

Let your blooming start from within, not from outside validation.

What If Blooming Looks Different for You?

Sometimes we picture blooming like a loud, colorful, confident transformation. But real blooming might look quieter:

Choosing not to argue when you're misunderstood

Returning to salah after weeks of struggling

Saying "Bismillah" before cooking

Crying in sujood because you finally feel safe again

Deciding to wear hijab — or to re-wear it after taking it off

These things matter.

These are blooms.

These are sacred victories only you and Allah fully understand.

Healing and Blooming Can Happen at the Same Time

You do not need to wait until you feel "fully healed" to do good, to feel joy, or to embrace hope.

The Prophet Muhammad ﷺ faced pain throughout his life — betrayal, grief, isolation — and yet his mercy, his worship, and his care for others never stopped. Why? Because blooming doesn't require the absence of pain. It requires turning to Allah through the pain.

You can cry in sajdah and still be blooming.

You can be unsure and still growing beautifully.

You can feel broken and still carry barakah.

You Are Not Behind

You're not too late.

You're not too far gone.

You're not disqualified because of your past.

Some of the most radiant gardens only bloom in their season. Not earlier. Not later. And when they do — they change the landscape.

That might be you.

Even if you feel hidden now, your time will come.

Even if you feel unsure now, Allah is preparing your heart.

Even if you feel tired now, your story isn't done.

Heart Reflection: A Du'a for This Chapter

Ya Allah…

If I'm holding myself back, help me release.

If I'm afraid of joy, help me welcome it.

If I've been hurt by people, help me remember You are not them.

Let me bloom at the pace You know is best.

Let my pain be the soil for something beautiful.

Let me trust that I don't need to be perfect to begin again.

Ameen.

Heart Journal 1:

"What part of yourself have you been hiding, waiting for the 'right time' to grow into? What would it look like to give yourself permission to bloom right where you are — not when you're perfect, not when others approve, but now?"

Write freely. Let this be a space where you uproot fear and plant courage instead.

Heart Journal 1

Heart Journal 1

CHAPTER 2
EMOTIONAL HEALING AS A FORM OF WORSHIP

Sometimes, the pain doesn't disappear just because you found the truth.

Reverting to Islam is beautiful — but it doesn't erase your past.

It doesn't make all the heartbreak, trauma, and confusion disappear overnight.

It doesn't mean your tears stop falling when you say La ilaha illAllah.

In fact, for many of us, that's when the real unraveling begins.

The Truth Can Be a Trigger

For some reverts, finding Islam brings peace and pressure all at once.

You finally have answers, but you also now have questions about everything you've been through:

Why did I suffer so much before I knew the truth?

Why do I still feel anxious, angry, or unworthy?

Am I allowed to take time to heal, or do I have to "move on" because I'm Muslim now?

Let me say this with love:

Healing is not a weakness. It's part of the worship.

The Heart Needs Time

The Prophet Muhammad ﷺ said:

"There is a piece of flesh in the body — if it is sound, the whole body is sound; and if it is corrupt, the whole body is corrupt. Verily, it is the heart."

(Sahih al-Bukhari)

Your heart is not a footnote in your journey. It's the center of it.

If your heart still carries wounds from abandonment, betrayal, loss, or trauma — know that tending to those wounds is part of tending to your relationship with Allah.

You can't force yourself to feel "fine." You can't shame yourself into spiritual wholeness.

You can heal. And you can do it slowly, as worship.

Healing Is Not Selfish

We sometimes believe that focusing on our emotional wellness is selfish. But in Islam, taking care of your heart — your emotional, mental, and spiritual core — is deeply rewarded.

Crying in du'a is healing.

Seeking therapy to understand your pain is healing.

Journaling what hurts and then making dhikr is healing.

Letting go of toxic people, even if it's painful, is healing.

Setting boundaries in the name of peace is healing.

All of this is part of worship — if you intend it for the sake of Allah and your wholeness.

What You Feel Is Not a Failure

You can love Allah and still feel sad.

You can trust Him and still feel scared.

You can believe in His plan and still feel grief over what didn't happen — or what did.

Don't let anyone tell you that "strong Muslims don't cry" or that "if you really had iman, you wouldn't feel like this."

Even the Prophets cried. Even the Prophet Muhammad ﷺ grieved. Even he sat with sadness when loved ones died, when his people rejected him, when he felt the weight of revelation.

What made him ﷺ strong was not that he never broke — but that he always turned to Allah when he did.

My Healing Was Not Linear

There were times I thought I had moved on. I was praying regularly, wearing a hijab, and reading books. From the outside, I was blooming. But some days, I would still cry without knowing why. Certain memories would surface and leave me aching. Some conversations would reopen old wounds I thought had closed.

And I felt ashamed. Why am I still hurting? Didn't I already find the truth?

But Allah was gentle with me.

Over time, I realized healing wasn't supposed to be fast.

It was layered. It was ongoing. It was honest.

And every time I brought my brokenness to Allah, He honored it.

Healing Can Look Like…

Sitting quietly after salah, just breathing, and letting your nervous system soften

Writing a letter you'll never send — and then making du'a for peace

Saying "No" without guilt to someone who used to manipulate you

Crying in sujood because it's the safest place your heart knows

Smiling again after thinking you never would

These are not distractions from your deen. They are your deen.

But What Will People Say?

As reverts, we sometimes worry that if we speak openly about our emotional struggles, others will question our faith.

But Allah never asked us to suffer in silence to appear righteous.

He asks us to turn to Him — in our struggles.

You don't need to prove your worthiness to anyone.

Healing is personal. Healing is sacred.

And you are allowed to take as long as you need.

Heart Reflection: A Du'a for This Chapter

Ya Allah…

Heal the parts of me I don't even have words for.

Let my heart become a place of peace — not just for others, but for myself.

Forgive me for the ways I've rushed or ignored my wounds.

Teach me to see healing as worship.

Let every tear, step, and du'a bring me closer to You.

And when I am whole, let me help others heal, too.

Ameen.

Heart Journal 2

What part of your emotional story still feels unhealed? Write about it — gently and without judgment.

How can you honor your healing today in a spiritually nourishing way?

Write a du'a to Allah using your own words — asking Him to hold your heart while it mends.

Heart Journal 2

CHAPTER 3

KEEPING FAITH WHEN YOU'RE SPIRITUALLY TIRED

You love Allah.

You believe in the truth of Islam.

You want to feel close to Him.

But lately… you're just tired.

Not physically — spiritually.

You're showing up for prayer, but it feels mechanical.

You're making du'a, but your heart isn't in it.

You want to feel inspired — but all you feel is flat. Quiet. Distant.

And you wonder, "What's wrong with me?"

But here's the truth: there is nothing wrong with you.

You are in a season of the soul that every believer faces.

Even the Heart Has Seasons

Like the moon waxes and wanes, like the tide flows and recedes, your iman will have highs and lows.

The Prophet Muhammad  acknowledged this when he said:

"Every act has a peak, and every peak is followed by a period of slackening. So, if one does it moderately and follows the sunnah during that period, he will succeed."

18

(Ahmad)

In other words, feeling spiritually tired doesn't make you a bad Muslim.

It makes you human.

And as long as you keep holding on — even if by a thread — you are still deeply loved by Allah.

It's Okay to Feel Numb Sometimes

You might miss the way your heart once raced at the sound of the adhan.

You might long for that spiritual high you felt when you first took shahada.

You might feel ashamed that you're going through the motions without emotion.

But Allah doesn't just reward your highs. He rewards your effort.

The prayer you make when you're exhausted still counts.

The dhikr you whisper with a tired heart still counts.

The fast you keep while feeling disconnected still counts.

And your willingness to keep going — despite the numbness — is beloved to Him.

What Causes Spiritual Fatigue?

Spiritual tiredness can come from many things:

Burnout from trying to do everything "right"

Emotional pain or unresolved trauma

Loneliness in your Muslim journey

Comparing yourself to others who seem more "righteous."

Neglecting self-care in the name of ibadah

Feeling unseen or unappreciated, even by fellow Muslims

Sometimes, we're carrying so much without realizing it. And faith, like any relationship, needs rest, reflection, and renewal.

My Season of Stillness

There was a time I felt spiritually blank. I was praying, reading, doing all the "right" things — but my heart felt heavy. I didn't feel connected. I felt guilty, like I was performing.

I even asked myself, "Am I losing my iman?"

But instead of quitting, I slowed down. I permitted myself to be with Allah instead of trying to impress Him.

I started praying slower. I stopped forcing extra acts of worship when my heart needed stillness. I sat in silence after salah, not to recite anything — to breathe.

And over time, the light came back.

Not suddenly. Not loudly. But gently.

Like the sun rising after a long night.

How to Nourish Your Faith Gently

You don't need a full spiritual "makeover." Sometimes, you need to soften:

Pray one prayer today with more presence, not pressure.

Read one ayah of Qur'an — and let it sit with you.

Make one heartfelt du'a without overthinking it.

Do one act of kindness to reconnect to Allah.

Say "Ya Allah, I miss You" — and let that be your worship.

You are not behind. You are simply in a slower chapter. And Allah is still with you.

You Don't Have to "Feel It" to Be Sincere

We often equate sincerity with emotion — tears, passion, longing. But sincerity is showing up even when those feelings are absent.

Allah doesn't ask for performance. He asks for presence.

Even if your presence is quiet.

Even if your mind drifts.

Even if your heart feels distant.

Keep returning. Keep showing up.

Because every time you do, you're saying, "Ya Allah, I haven't given up."

And that means everything.

Let Go of the Pressure to Be "On Fire"

Sometimes, our spiritual fatigue comes from trying to do everything perfectly.

Every sunnah.

Every du'a.

Every lecture.

Every fasting day.

And while all of these are beautiful, Islam is not meant to burn you out.

The Prophet Muhammad ﷺ said:

"The most beloved deeds to Allah are those done consistently, even small ones."

(Bukhari)

If you need to scale back to protect your heart — do so. That's not failure. That's wisdom.

Faith Will Return — Even If Slowly

If your soul feels dry right now, trust that this isn't the end of your spiritual story.

Ask Allah to revive your heart.

Keep doing the basics.

And trust that your faith is not gone — just resting.

Sometimes the most powerful thing you can say is:

"Ya Allah, I'm tired. But I still choose You."

And He hears that. He honors that. And He will carry you through.

Heart Reflection: A Du'a for This Chapter

Ya Allah…

My heart feels distant, but I'm still Yours.

I'm tired — not from You, but from trying so hard to be "perfect."

Give me space to rest without guilt.

Remind me that You love effort, not just energy.

Let me feel Your closeness, even when I can't feel much at all.

Let me trust that You are still near — even when I feel far.

Ameen.

Heart Journal 3

When was the last time you felt deeply connected in your faith? What was different then?

What are 1–2 gentle, sustainable ways you can nourish your iman this week?

Write a letter to Allah beginning with: "Ya Allah, I know I'm tired, but…"

Heart Journal 3

Heart Journal 3

CHAPTER 4
WHAT BEAUTIFUL PATIENCE TAUGHT ME

"Indeed, Allah is with the patient."— Surah Al-Baqarah (2:153)

Sometimes, Allah doesn't change your situation right away—because He's changing *you* first.

The Qur'an shows us how Prophet Yusuf, peace be upon him, endured betrayal, false accusations, abandonment, and years of silence before his story bloomed into relief and honor. But he didn't just wait. He trusted.

And so did his father, Ya'qub, peace be upon him who said:

"So patience is most fitting (*fa-sabrun jamil*). And Allah is the one sought for help against what you describe." (Surah Yusuf, 12:18)

When I went through one of the hardest tests of my life, I felt like everything I had built was falling apart. The silence of that chapter felt endless. The loneliness—loud, one that left me feeling emptied and alone. I didn't have answers, but I had a sticky note.

I didn't have many words. But I wrote one: **"Patience."** I stuck it on my fridge. And every year that passed, I added the date underneath.

2009.

2010.

2011.

2012.

By 2013, I went to add the next year… but the note was full. No more space. And what I didn't know then — was that 2013 would be the year I'd marry Mohamed. My partner. My best friend. The one who helped me believe in softness again. The one who brought joy back into my du'as. The completion of my deen… again.

But here's the truth: the most beautiful part of that journey wasn't the ending — it was what I discovered *during* it.

I found S*abr*, patience.

Not the kind you fake when people ask if you're okay. Not the kind that grits its teeth in silence. But the kind that blooms from surrender. The kind that gently whispers, *"My Lord is subtle in what He wills." Sabrun jamil.* Beautiful patience. Not bitter. Not performative. Just faithful. Soft. Still.

Your Yusuf moment may still be unfolding. You may still be at the edge of your own reunion, or healing, or relief. But never doubt this: What's ahead may be more beautiful than what was taken. And even if it isn't… what you *find in the waiting* might be the greatest gift of all.

I didn't know Allah was preparing something for me. But more importantly… He was preparing *me.*

Heart Reflection: The Beautiful Patience of Prophet Yusuf, peace be upon him.

Sometimes the pain feels unfair. The waiting feels endless. The silence from the world feels heavy.

But then you remember prophet Yusuf, peace be upon him.

He was betrayed by his own brothers. Thrown into a well. Sold as a slave. Falsely accused. Imprisoned. Forgotten.

And still… he held onto his dignity. Still… he whispered to His Lord. Still… he waited with hope.

His father, Prophet Ya'qub, peace be upon him, whose heart broke at the loss of his son, said:

He didn't know when or how relief would come. But he believed it would.

Years later, when Yusuf, peace be upon him, stood in a place of power and reunion, he didn't let ego speak. He simply said:

"Indeed, my Lord is subtle in what He wills. Indeed, it is He who is the Knowing, the Wise." (Surah Yusuf, 12:100)

That is *Sabrun jamil* — beautiful patience. Not bitter. Not resentful. Just quiet trust that Allah never forgets.

This is the beauty of his story: it reminds us that the road may twist, and justice may be delayed, but nothing is ever wasted. No tear. No prayer. No chapter of your life that feels lost.

A Du'a for This Chapter

Ya Allah, When I feel abandoned, remind me of Prophet Yusuf. When I feel delayed, remind me of Prophet Ya'qub. Let me trust that You never waste pain. Soften my heart with sabrun jamil. Let me walk through my trials with grace, and meet Your wisdom in the unfolding.

If I must wait, let it not harden me. Let it soften me. Let it teach me the quiet art of beautiful patience. Let my heart trust in Your subtle plan, Even when I can't see the ending. Let my story bloom in Your perfect timing.

Heart Journal 4

Think back to a time when you were waiting for something you deeply longed for. What did you learn in the silence between the du'a and the answer?

Write about how that waiting shaped you — not just what you received, but who you became in the waiting.

Heart Journal 4

Heart Journal 4

CHAPTER 5

THE DAY YOU REALIZED YOU WERE MUSLIM FOR LIFE

There comes a moment — subtle, quiet — when you realize this isn't temporary.

This isn't a phase.

You're not "trying out" Islam anymore.

You're living it.

It might not happen the day you say your shahada.

It might not happen after your first Ramadan.

It might not even be when you memorize your first surah or start praying five times a day.

But one day, you'll be walking through your daily routine — pouring tea, answering messages, folding laundry — and you'll catch yourself whispering "Bismillah" before you begin.

You'll say "Alhamdulillah" after a sigh.

You'll instinctively make du'a when you lose something, or when the sky turns pink, or when your heart starts aching.

And in that moment, it hits you:

This isn't something you're trying to become anymore.

This is who you are.

You're Muslim.

And not just legally, or socially, or technically.

But deep in your bones. Quiet in your breath. Steady in your soul.

You've built a life where your faith is not decoration.

It's foundation.

You've learned to love Allah in your own language.

You've stumbled and still returned to Him.

You've questioned, grieved, healed, and stayed.

You've made Islam your home — even if no one else in your family has.

Even if you still forget an ayah.

Even if your Arabic isn't fluent.

Even if you still feel like you're learning every single day.

You're not on the outside anymore.

You're planted.

And no matter what happens from here — this is your root.

This is your forever.

Heart Reflection: When Islam Becomes Who You Are

You don't need to prove anything to anyone.

The real proof is in your consistency.

In your quiet worship.

In the way, you turn to Allah when life hits hard.

Being Muslim for life doesn't mean never struggling.

It means never leaving — even when you struggle.

A Du'a for the Day You Knew

Ya Allah, You found me when I didn't know I was searching. You called my heart when the world felt too loud. And I said yes — not always with strength, but with sincerity.

Let me never forget the moment I knew I was Yours — not just by name, but by soul. When Islam became not a phase or a feeling, but home.

Ya Rabb, Make me firm upon this path. Even when I tremble, let my heart stay close to You. Let my Islam be a light I carry — in ease, in hardship, in silence, in joy. Let it grow roots in every breath of my being, until I meet You with a heart that whispers: "I chose You, again and again."

Ameen.

Heart Journal 5

When did you first feel like Islam was no longer "new" — but part of your daily rhythm?

Write a note to your future self, five years from now, still walking this path. What do you want her to remember?

Heart Journal 5

Heart Journal 5

PART II

RECLAIMING JOY, IDENTITY, AND BELONGING

CHAPTER 6

RECLAIMING JOY AS A MUSLIM

Somewhere along the way, joy became something we thought we had to give up.

Maybe you were told that being a "good Muslim" means always being serious.

Maybe you were made to feel guilty for smiling too much, laughing out loud, or enjoying simple things like music, nature, or a moment of silliness.

Maybe you internalized the idea that joy was dangerous — a distraction from the akhirah.

But the truth is: Islam does not ask you to shrink your joy.

It simply asks you to anchor it in what's halal, in what pleases Allah — and in what brings lasting benefit to your heart.

Joy, when rooted in faith, is not selfish. It's a form of gratitude.

The Prophet Muhammad  and Joy

The Prophet Muhammad ﷺ was not a man of constant severity.

Yes, he cried in prayer. Yes, he felt the weight of his mission. But he also laughed. He smiled often. He played with children. He raced his wife. He celebrated victories with his companions.

He didn't live a life void of joy — he lived a life full of purposeful joy.

And if he ﷺ found time to smile in the face of hardship, to enjoy halal moments of lightness, and to encourage others to do the same — then so can we.

Joy Is Not a Distraction — It's a Sign of Life

As reverts, many of us come into Islam with seriousness. We feel we've been given this precious truth, and we don't want to mess it up. That sense of responsibility is beautiful — but it can also become heavy if we don't let in light.

Sometimes we feel like we must always be "doing better," and we forget to just be.

Joy doesn't mean abandoning your pursuit of righteousness.

Joy means making room for the mercy of Allah to live in your day — not just in theory.

It can be as simple as:

Laughing with a friend who supports your deen

Going on a walk and feeling the breeze as a sign of Allah's mercy

Cooking your favorite halal meal and saying Alhamdulillah with each bite

Playing a silly game with your child and realizing it's a kind of worship too

Joy that is conscious, halal, and mindful — is not forbidden. It is beloved.

Unlearning Guilt Around Joy

Many of us carry shame from past experiences — maybe we partied, overindulged, or chased happiness in unhealthy ways before Islam. So now, even when something is clearly permissible, we question whether we're "going back" or doing something wrong.

Let me remind you:

Halal joy is not a regression. It's renewal.

It's you learning how to feel whole again — in a way that honors Allah.

The joy that Islam brings is not empty. It's rooted. It's not fleeting. It leaves peace behind it.

But that joy can only flourish if we give ourselves permission to feel it.

Real Talk: Joy Can Feel Scary

It might sound strange, but sometimes we're afraid to be joyful.

When we've been hurt, when life has been unstable, when faith has been tested — joy can feel unsafe. We worry it won't last. We think if we let ourselves enjoy something, the pain will just come back stronger later.

This is where trusting Allah comes in.

Joy is not a betrayal of your past wounds. It's a sign that healing is possible.

Joy is not naivety — it's courage.

Joy says: I believe Allah can write something beautiful for me, even after everything.

Your Joy Can Be Dawah

When others see you joyful — not in rebellion, but in remembrance — they see Islam differently.

They see a deen that doesn't just restrict, but uplifts.

They see a Muslim who isn't just disciplined but fulfilled.

They see faith that brings peace and purpose — not pressure and performance.

Your halal joy is a form of dawah. It's a quiet way of saying:

"I have found something so whole, so healing, that even my smile remembers Allah."

Joy Looks Different for Everyone

Maybe your joy is quiet — tea and Qur'an in a corner of your home.

Maybe it's creative — painting, writing, crafting beautiful things with barakah in your hands.

Maybe it's communal — Eid parties, laughter with sisters, family dinners.

Maybe it's active — walks, travel, movement that makes you say SubhanAllah at every turn.

Whatever your joy looks like, reclaim it. Reclaim it from guilt. Reclaim it from fear.

And let it be a bridge that brings you closer to your Lord.

Heart Reflection: A Du'a for This Chapter

Ya Allah…

Let me love this life without losing sight of the next.

Let my joy be worship, not distraction.

Let me smile with gratitude, not guilt.

Heal me from the fear that happiness will be taken away.

Teach me that halal joy is from You.

And when I laugh, when I dance in private, when I breathe in peace —

let it all be a form of dhikr.

Ameen.

Heart Journal 6

What are some halal joys in your life that you've been afraid to fully enjoy? Why?

What brings you light — not just happiness, but the kind that stays with you?

What would reclaiming joy as a Muslim look like in this season of your life?

Heart Journal 6

CHAPTER 7

THE BEAUTY OF HALAL CELEBRATION

Do you remember your first Eid?

Maybe you didn't know what to expect.

Maybe you dressed up with quiet nervousness, not knowing if you'd fit in.

Maybe you spent it alone — unsure how to celebrate, unsure who to call, unsure if you were even allowed to feel excited.

As reverts, our celebrations don't always begin with a bang. Sometimes they begin with a whisper — a longing to feel joy that's both genuine and grounded in our new faith.

But slowly, over time, we learn:

Islam loves celebration.

And halal joy isn't just allowed — it's rewarded.

Celebrating What Allah Loves

The Prophet Muhammad  said:

"The people of every nation have their festival, and this is our festival."

(Sahih al-Bukhari)

Islam gave us Eid as a response to ibadah — to our fasting, our patience, our prayers, our sacrifice. It wasn't meant to be quiet or hidden. It was meant to be shared, bright, joyful, full of takbeer and thankfulness.

You are not wrong for wanting to celebrate. You're honoring your deen by doing so.

Rewriting What Celebration Looks Like

For many reverts, celebration was once tied to things we've left behind: loud parties, alcohol, music that fed our pain instead of healing it.

So now, we're unsure what celebration means. We're afraid we'll get it wrong.

But halal celebration is more than what's "not allowed." It's about what is beautifully allowed:

Wearing your favorite outfit to mark the day

Sharing sweets and meals with friends or neighbors

Decorating your space with lights, flowers, or heartfelt reminders of faith

Giving gifts with sincerity, not extravagance

Laughing together in remembrance of Allah

These things don't "water down" our faith. They breathe life into it.

Your Joy Can Be Gentle and Deep

Halal celebration doesn't mean turning your home into a carnival. Unless that's what brings your heart joy — then go for it.

But for others, celebration may look like:

Quiet reflection after completing Ramadan

A small get-together with close friends who see your deen

Making a meal your mother once cooked, and saying Bismillah as you reclaim it with new meaning

Crying from joy that you made it — another Ramadan, another prayer, another Eid

You don't need a crowd to celebrate. You just need presence.

Making New Traditions (Even If You Start Alone)

One of the hardest parts of being a revert is that holidays often feel lonely.

You may not have a Muslim family.

You may be the only one taking it seriously.

You may miss the chaotic joy you once had — even if it came from a different belief system.

But here's something hopeful:

You get to make new traditions.

You get to start small — baking something you love, making du'a at sunrise, calling another sister, gifting your child a handwritten note.

And over time, these moments layer into something sacred.

They become your way of saying, "These matters. This day is from Allah. And I honor it."

Even if no one else understands — He does.

My First Eid

I still remember my first Eid. I was excited, but unsure. I didn't grow up with henna or gift bags or prayer at the masjid. I had no idea what to wear or how to act. And while I saw smiles around me, I felt a little bit out of place.

But I smiled anyway. I made du'a anyway. I wore my best scarf, even if it felt stiff and new. I went to the prayer and watched the waves of Muslims embrace each other, say "Taqabbal Allahu minna wa minkum," and cheer their kids with joy.

I didn't know how to fully participate — but I knew this was beautiful.

And I whispered, Ya Allah, let me learn to love this too.

You Deserve to Feel Included

Maybe you don't have a big group of Muslim friends.

Maybe you're still figuring out how to make halal fun.

Maybe part of you still grieves the loss of other holidays and gatherings you used to know.

That's okay.

Islam doesn't erase your past. It redefines your future.

You can carry joy in your new identity without shame. You can make space for your own unique way of celebrating. You can honor Eid, weddings, baby showers, new beginnings — all within the beauty of halal.

And you can trust that each time you celebrate in a way that pleases Allah, He is pleased with you.

Heart Reflection: A Du'a for This Chapter

Ya Allah…

Teach me how to celebrate what You love.

Let me feel included in the joy of this ummah.

Replace old memories with new ones full of light.

Let me celebrate with presence, with purpose, and with peace.

Let me not compare my path to others.

Let me bloom in my own rhythm — and smile with sincerity.

Ameen.

Heart Journal 7

What did celebration mean to you before Islam?

What would a halal version of that look like now?

Write down 3 ways you can make your next Eid feel joyful — even if it's small, even if you're on your own.

Heart Journal 7

Heart Journal 7

CHAPTER 8

LAUGHING WITHOUT GUILT — LIGHTNESS IN ISLAM

Somewhere along the way, many of us picked up the belief that piety and playfulness cannot coexist.

That to be serious about Islam, we must always be serious in demeanor. That laughter is frivolous. That jokes and joy must be kept in check — or avoided altogether. Especially for women. Especially for Muslims.

But here's the gentle truth you may need to hear again:

Islam is a religion of balance.

And part of that balance is joy.

Lightness. Smiling. Laughing — even playfully.

The Prophet Muhammad  Smiled Often.

One of the most well-documented characteristics of the Prophet Muhammad is that he smiled—a lot. His companions described him as rarely being stern unless necessary. His face carried serenity and ease. His laughter was not excessive or loud, but it was sincere.

He raced his wife. He teased his companions in kind ways. He made people feel comfortable.

He didn't frown his way through life to prove his taqwa.

He showed us that lightness can be prophetic.

When We Carry Too Much Guilt

Many of us reverts come from a background where joy may have been connected to things we no longer feel comfortable with: music, parties, inappropriate humor, or mockery. So now, we tread lightly. We become unsure. We wonder if laughter still fits into this new life.

We might find ourselves holding back a smile. Or biting our tongue from a harmless joke. Or silencing a burst of laughter because it feels wrong — even when it's not.

This is often more about unhealed fear than fiqh.

You are not betraying your faith by being lighthearted.

You are not less righteous because you laughed at a funny moment with a friend.

And you do not have to carry guilt for every sound of joy your soul releases.

You Were Created with Emotions — Not Against Them

Allah created your heart with the ability to laugh and cry, to feel delight and sorrow, to swing between stillness and silliness.

He could have made you stoic and cold. But He didn't.

The Prophet Muhammad ﷺ didn't just tolerate emotions. He honored them, welcomed their presence, and redirected them when needed—without shame.

You don't need to perform piety through a poker face. You need to live your piety with sincerity, including the moments that make you laugh so hard you lose your breath.

Lightness Is a Form of Trust

Sometimes, we become so consumed by the world's heaviness — war, injustice, sadness, and spiritual struggle — that laughter feels irresponsible. How can we laugh when others are suffering? How can we enjoy a silly moment while still learning so much?

But even in the darkest times, lightness can be resistance. It can be worship.

To allow yourself to laugh — when you know the world is imperfect, when your faith is still forming — is not denial. It is a quiet act of trust in Allah.

It says: Ya Allah, I know You are still in control. I know I can feel joy even while I grow.

Faith Doesn't Have to Be Heavy All the Time

Sometimes faith feels like weight: the pressure to pray, the guilt of missing a sunnah, the confusion over rulings, the anxiety of getting things right.

But faith can also feel like relief—like a breath in, like a shared joke with a sister who gets your journey, like being able to say "Alhamdulillah" after a long day and really mean it.

Laughter reminds us that life is still unfolding, that blessings are still coming, and that not everything needs to be figured out before we allow ourselves to feel good.

When You're the "Funny One"

If you've always been the funny one — the storyteller, the comic relief, the one who brings smiles — maybe you've wondered if there's space for that version of you in Islam.

The answer is: yes, with intention.

If your humor doesn't mock, harm, or distract from remembrance, it can be a mercy. Your lightness can be healing for others. And when rooted in sincerity, it can be worship.

There's no need to become someone you're not. Just let your laughter carry barakah, not baggage. Let it come from the heart, not the ego. And let it serve others in kindness, not sarcasm.

There were times I wondered if I had to change my entire personality to be taken seriously as a Muslim. I loved to laugh. I found joy in storytelling, awkward moments, and beauty in ordinary things.

At one point, I felt I had to trade all that in for a more "serious" tone. But over time, I realized that my laughter didn't take me away from Islam — it brought me closer.

It was my way of softening the hard edges. Of connecting with others. Of surviving tough seasons.

And when I did it for the sake of connection, not ego — I knew it was something Allah didn't just allow. He blessed it.

Heart Reflection: A Du'a for This Chapter

Ya Allah…

Make my laughter a reminder of Your mercy.

Keep my joy rooted in gratitude, not heedlessness.

Let me be a source of light for others — through my smile, my stories, my sincerity.

Free me from the guilt of joy.

Teach me to honor the balance You placed in my heart.

Let me live lightly, love deeply, and laugh sincerely — all for You. Ameen.

Heart Journal 8

What moments make you laugh from the soul? Write one down and thank Allah for it.

Have you ever felt guilty about being too lighthearted? Where did that belief come from?

How can you bring more joy daily without compromising your faith?

Heart Journal 8

Heart Journal 8

CHAPTER 9

RELEARNING HOW TO CELEBRATE — JOY IN HALAL WAYS

You might've grown up with birthdays, holidays, or weekend parties that defined celebration.

Lights, music, big dinners, clinking glasses — a kind of joy that felt familiar.

Then you embraced Islam… and joy started to feel more complicated.

You asked yourself:

Can I still dance? Laugh? Celebrate life?

Am I allowed to enjoy things the way I used to?

Sometimes, it felt like the joy was gone — or at least hidden.

But over time, you learn that joy isn't haram. It's sacred — when done in ways that honor Allah.

The Myth That Faith Means Restriction

One of the biggest misconceptions new Muslims struggle with is the idea that Islam is "serious," but not joyful.

But joy is part of the deen.

The Prophet Muhammad ﷺ smiled often.

He joked with his companions (without lying).

He celebrated Eid with poetry, food, and festivity.

He attended weddings.

While Aisha watched, he even let Abyssinian men perform with spears in the masjid courtyard.

Islam doesn't erase celebration.

It refines it.

It redirects it from temporary highs… to deep, fulfilling, soul-safe joy.

What Joy Looks Like in Islam

It may look a little different — and that's okay.

It may take time to adjust — and that's okay too.

Joy in Islam can look like:

A home full of laughter and dhikr

A halal party with games and dessert and heartfelt du'a

A wedding where haya (modesty) and happiness both shine

A hike with friends, marveling at Allah's creation

An Eid brunch with your favorite foods, dressed in your best

Gift-giving with intention, not extravagance

Eating together while saying Bismillah and Alhamdulillah

This is joy.

It's halal.

And it's beautiful.

Learning New Ways to Celebrate

As a revert, you may feel unsure. You might even grieve the way you used to celebrate.

And that's normal.

You can honor those memories without holding onto the parts that don't serve your faith.

You can say goodbye to what no longer aligns — and say Bismillah to a new kind of joy.

This joy doesn't numb — it nourishes.

It doesn't push you toward regret — it fills you with barakah.

And best of all? You don't need to recover from it the next day.

My Journey with Relearning Joy

There was a time I thought being religious meant being reserved all the time.

I tried to quiet my laughter, limit my expressions, avoid too much "fun."

But it didn't feel authentic. It felt heavy.

Over time, I began to let go of that false idea.

I hosted Eid potlucks.

I laughed with sisters with fun games — our hearts full of shared faith.

I decorated my home with lights and banners during Ramadan.

And I realized:

Islam didn't take joy from me. It brought me back to real, soul-safe joy.

When You Feel Left Out

Sometimes, your family or friends will celebrate in ways you no longer join.

And that can make you feel left out — or judged.

You don't have to criticize them.

You don't have to isolate yourself completely.

But you can set gentle boundaries while still showing love.

And when you feel lonely, remind yourself:

You've traded the fleeting for the forever.

And Allah will never let you lose something for His sake without giving you better.

How to Bring Halal Joy Into Your Life

Mark your Eids like you mean it.

Dress up. Host. Exchange gifts. Start your own traditions.

Celebrate milestones with intention.

A new job? A goal reached? Bake something and say Alhamdulillah.

Plan outings that feed your soul.

Nature walks. Game nights. Beach picnics. Masjid meetups.

Laugh. Without guilt.

The Prophet Muhammad ﷺ smiled and laughed with his companions. You can too.

Invite others into your joy.

Reverts, children, elders — make your celebrations feel like home.

Joy Is Part of Worship

Joy doesn't pull you away from Allah — when it's rooted in gratitude, it brings you closer.

Saying Alhamdulillah over a good meal.

Saying SubhanAllah when you see a beautiful sunset.

Saying Bismillah before you start the fun.

These are acts of worship too.

Don't let anyone convince you that Islam is about suppressing your spirit.

The Prophet Muhammad ﷺ brought lightness, laughter, and love — all wrapped in modesty and mercy.

Heart Reflection: A Du'a for This Chapter

Ya Allah…

Let me experience the joy You made halal for me.

Let my celebrations be full of gratitude and remembrance.

Help me let go of past habits without bitterness.

Teach me to celebrate life in ways that bring me closer to You.

Let my joy be a light for others.

Let it remind me that You are the Giver of delight,

and that every moment of sweetness is a gift from You.

Ameen.

Heart Journal 9

What's one joyful memory you've had since becoming Muslim? What made it feel pure?

What's something you miss about how you used to celebrate — and how might you replace it in a halal way?

What new traditions or celebrations would you like to create in your life or with others?

Heart Journal 9

Heart Journal 9

CHAPTER 10

WHEN YOU NO LONGER HIDE THAT YOU'RE MUSLIM

It often starts small.

You could tuck your prayer beads into your pocket when coworkers walk by.

Maybe you lower your voice when saying As-salaam 'Alaykum on the phone.

Maybe you hesitate before pulling your prayer mat out at the airport or delay your salah to avoid stares.

As reverts, many of us know what it's like to carry our Islam in pieces — quietly, cautiously, like a beautiful gift we're afraid others will reject.

And then, one day… something shifts.

You stop hiding.

You say Bismillah before eating in public.

You wear hijab without looking around to see who's watching.

You excuse yourself at a family gathering to pray — not in secret, but with gentle confidence.

You are no longer performing to be accepted.

You're simply… Muslim.

From Fear to Freedom

It doesn't happen overnight. For some of us, it takes months or even years. There may be a moment, or many moments, when you quietly choose truth over comfort.

Maybe it's the first time you say you don't shake hands — and you're ready for the awkwardness.

Maybe it's explaining Ramadan to your boss and not watering it down.

Maybe it's updating your social media profile picture in hijab, even if you know people from your past will see it.

And maybe — just maybe — you feel scared... and proud... at the same time.

That's what courage looks like.

Why We Hide in the First Place

Let's be honest. It's not just about safety. Sometimes, it's about shame. About wanting to avoid judgment, awkwardness, or being "the weird one."

Maybe your family still doesn't understand why you converted.

Maybe your coworkers assume Islam is oppressive or extreme.

Maybe you worry you're not "good enough" to represent Islam in the first place.

But here's what you need to remember:

Your faith is not a performance.

It's a relationship.

It's not about always saying the perfect thing — *it's about showing up sincerely.*

And you are allowed to exist as a Muslim, out loud, even if you're still growing.

The Day I Stopped Hiding

For the first time, I found myself scanning menus differently—not for calories or cravings—but for certainty. I wanted to ensure the food being served had no pork. It sounds small, but to me, it wasn't. It was one of those quiet, internal shifts that signaled, *"I am Muslim now."*

But I didn't announce it out loud. I just politely asked the waiter or quietly chose a different dish. My heart beat a little faster each time, not because of the food but because of what it meant: that I was beginning to live this faith—even in simple, unseen ways.

I remember choosing to pray at a rest stop on a road trip — in front of everyone, not tucked behind a vending machine. I was nervous, but I felt at peace.

I remember posting an ayah on social media — not for show, but because it spoke to my heart. And I let people from my "before Islam" life see it.

Those moments weren't loud. But they were mine. They were sacred.

And they were signs: I am no longer hiding.

Visibility Is Not Vanity

You don't wear your Islam outwardly to impress others.

You do it because it's part of who you are.

You do it because it brings barakah. Because it invites conversations. Because it reminds you to carry yourself with integrity — even when no one's watching.

Yes, you may get stares.

Yes, you may get awkward questions.

But you may also inspire someone, plant a seed, find someone else who was hiding, and help them feel seen.

Hijab, Prayer, and Public Identity

For sisters especially, wearing the hijab can be the biggest shift. It's not just cloth—it's a statement—one that you didn't ask to be politicized but one that now shapes how people see you.

And it's okay if that feels heavy at first.

It's okay if you take time to grow into that public visibility.

But know this: every time you step out as your Muslim self, it's an act of strength. Not because of the eyes watching — but because of the intention behind it.

Allah sees.

Allah knows what it costs you.

And Allah honors that courage.

Claiming Your Space

You are allowed to pray in a public place.

You are allowed to wear clothes that align with your modesty.

You are allowed to ask if the food has gelatin.

You are allowed to say "Alhamdulillah" when someone sneezes — even in a waiting room, classroom, or office meeting.

You do not need to shrink to make others comfortable.

You can carry your faith with kindness. With humility. With ease.

And you can do it without hiding.

And If You Still Hide Sometimes...

That's okay.

This isn't about perfection. It's about becoming.

We all have moments when we pull back when we don't correct someone, when we whisper instead of speak when we choose comfort over conviction.

Don't shame yourself for that.

Just notice it. Grow through it.

And ask Allah to make you bold — not for pride, but for His pleasure.

Heart Reflection: A Du'a for This Chapter

Ya Allah…

Make me brave in my identity.

Let me walk in this world as a Muslim — with peace, not fear.

Remove the need for approval from my heart.

When I hide, bring me back.

When I feel small, remind me that I am Yours.

Let my visibility be a quiet dawah, and my presence be a reflection of Your mercy.

Ameen.

Heart Journal 10

What were some of the small ways you used to "hide" your Islam — in dress, food choices, or conversations?

(There is no shame in the past. This is a place to witness your growth with compassion.)

CHAPTER 11

WALKING PROUDLY WITH YOUR IMAN (FAITH)

There is a quiet confidence that comes when you no longer shrink your faith.

Not arrogance. Not performance.

But a steady knowing — that you are guided, and that this guidance is a gift.

That's what it means to walk proudly with your iman.

It doesn't mean you never struggle.

It means your struggles don't make you doubt your place with Allah.

It means you carry your identity not with apology — but with peace.

From Shaky Steps to Steady Strides

In the beginning, many of us tread carefully. We're unsure how much to share, how much to do, or whether we're doing it right. Our image feels fragile — like it could crack under pressure or be exposed as inadequate.

But slowly, something shifts. You catch yourself saying "Alhamdulillah" without thinking. You correct someone's misconception about Islam — not to argue, but with grace. You walk into the masjid and feel like you belong.

Your faith has moved from your lips into your limbs. Into your choices. Into your rhythm.

That's when you start walking proudly — not for others to see you, but because you finally see yourself.

Confidence Without Comparison

Walking with Iman doesn't mean looking down on others. It means lifting your gaze from their paths and focusing on your own.

Confidence in Islam is not about knowing more Arabic, having memorized more surahs, or checking more boxes.

It's about:

Knowing your worth is defined by Allah

Living by what you believe, even when it's inconvenient

Feeling comfortable saying "I don't know" — but still showing up

Choosing obedience when no one else is watching

That kind of quiet, unshakable faith is not loud but powerful.

"But I Still Feel Insecure Sometimes…"

So do all of us.

Walking proudly doesn't mean you never feel awkward. It means you keep walking anyway.

You can still feel out of place at the masjid. You can still mispronounce Arabic words. You can still forget a du'a mid-prayer and feel flustered. And yet — you're still walking. You're still showing up.

That is the kind of pride Allah loves. Not ego. Not self-righteousness. But a heart that is resilient in the face of doubt.

Let Your Faith Be Seen

There is something beautiful about seeing someone walk with quiet conviction.

It's in the way a sister adjusts her hijab with dignity — not defensiveness.

It's in the way a brother pauses everything for salah, even during busy work hours.

It's in the way a revert says, "I'm Muslim," without a pause, even when asked by someone who won't understand.

Let your actions reflect the light in your heart.

Let your faith be visible — not for attention, but for sincerity.

You never know who is watching and drawing strength from your example.

My Turning Point

There came a time when I stopped needing others to affirm my choices.

When I wore my identity without flinching. When I no longer questioned whether I "fit in" among born Muslims or felt like I had to explain myself at every turn.

It wasn't pride. It was peace.

A deep, internal knowing that I am Muslim. I am trying. I am enough.

Not because I was doing everything perfectly.

But because I had chosen Allah — and kept choosing Him, again and again.

What Walking Proudly Isn't

It's not:

Being loud for the sake of being noticed

Shaming others for being at different stages

Flaunting knowledge without humility

Pretending to have no questions or weak moments

True pride in faith comes with gentleness, humility, and compassion.

The Prophet Muhammad ﷺ was described as rahmah—mercy. His strength came with softness, and his dignity came with grace.

Iman Is an Inner Light

You don't need to convince anyone of your sincerity.

You don't need to carry proof of your devotion.

Your iman is between you and Allah — but the way you walk with it…

The way it changes how you speak, how you react, how you hold space for others…

That's the legacy of someone whose heart is anchored in something eternal.

That's what it means to walk with Iman.

Heart Reflection: A Du'a for This Chapter

Ya Allah…

Let my iman be steady and sincere.

Let it shape how I walk through this world — not with arrogance, but with confidence.

Let me move with purpose, not performance.

Keep my heart firm in the face of pressure.

And when I stumble, bring me back — gently, lovingly, fully.

Let others see You in me, not for praise, but as a reflection of Your mercy.

Ameen.

Heart Journal 11

What does "walk proudly with your iman" mean in your own life?

Write about a moment when you felt firm and unapologetic in your Muslim identity.

Heart Journal 11

Heart Journal 11

CHAPTER 12
ANSWERING QUESTIONS WITH GRACE

"So… why did you convert?"

"Do you really have to wear that?"

"Do you sleep with the scarf on?"

"Wait, you can't even have water during Ramadan?"

"Isn't Islam really strict?"

"Do you still celebrate Christmas?"

"Oh… you're not allowed to date?"

If you've heard any of these questions, welcome to the club.

As reverts, we often become "the Muslim they know." That one friend, co-worker, neighbor, or family member who now unintentionally represents an entire religion in the eyes of others.

And it can feel like a lot.

But here's the good news:

You don't need to have all the answers.

You need to answer with grace.

You Are Not a Spokesperson for Perfection

Sometimes we think, "If I say the wrong thing, they'll misunderstand Islam forever."

Or, "If I don't know the answer, I'll look weak in my faith."

But your job is not to be flawless.

Your job is to be real.

To answer what you can, with sincerity. To admit what you don't know. And to let your character fill in the blanks your words can't cover.

You're not speaking on behalf of every Muslim. You're just offering your window — your journey, your heart, your sincerity.

And that's powerful enough.

When Curiosity Feels Like Criticism

Sometimes, questions come from a good place. But they can still feel invasive or exhausting.

You may feel caught off guard.

You may worry about being mocked.

You may wonder, "Why do I have to explain myself at all?"

And you're allowed to feel that way.

But grace doesn't mean you always have to answer. Grace means you respond in a way that honors Allah — whether that's with kindness, wisdom, boundaries, or a peaceful, "That's something I'm still learning too."

Scripts to Keep in Your Pocket

Here are a few gentle ways to respond when you're unsure what to say:

"That's a great question. I don't have a full answer, but I'd love to look into it more."

"There's actually a lot of depth to that — would you like me to send you a video or article later?"

"I'm still growing in my understanding too. Islam encourages us to keep learning."

"I've found peace in this, even if it's not what most people expect."

You don't need to debate. You don't need to defend. You need to show that Islam is lived — not just explained.

Sharing Without Oversharing

Sometimes we feel obligated to tell our whole story every time someone asks why we became Muslim.

But your story is yours. You can protect it, share pieces of it, or none at all.

You are not being dishonest by offering a simplified answer like:

"Islam gave me the peace I was missing."

Sometimes that's enough. Sometimes that opens a door. And sometimes silence says more than an essay ever could.

And When the Questions Hurt…

Some questions aren't innocent.

Some people ask just to argue. Just to belittle. Just to provoke.

You don't have to entertain that energy.

You are allowed to say:

"I'm not comfortable discussing that."

"That question feels a little disrespectful."

"Let's change the topic."

Or to smile and walk away.

Even the Prophet Muhammad ﷺ stayed silent when taunted. Grace doesn't mean passivity. It means responding from a place of calm self-respect — not ego, not anger, not fear.

You Are Still Learning Too

Don't be embarrassed if you fumble through answers.

Don't hide if you Google something after someone asks.

Don't feel ashamed if you change your answer later after gaining clarity.

That's not failure — that's faith in motion.

Islam is a lifelong learning curve. No one has it all figured out. The more you grow, the more your answers will deepen — and so will your confidence.

Let your sincerity shine through. People remember that more than perfect phrasing.

The Best Dawah Is Character

You may forget the hadith reference.

You may misquote an ayah.

You may say "I think" more times than you want to.

But when people see you respond with kindness, composure, and humility — that's dawah. That's planting seeds.

They may not convert, and they may not even agree, but they'll remember that the Muslim they met was thoughtful, respectful, and rooted.

And that memory can outlive any debate.

A Moment I Remember

Someone once asked me, "So, do you really believe all of it? Like… all the rules and stuff?"

I paused, unsure what to say.

Then I replied, "I believe in Allah. And that belief helps me understand the rest — even the things I'm still learning to accept."

They didn't ask anything else. But their expression softened.

And I realized that grace had done what argument never could.

Heart Reflection: A Du'a for This Chapter

Ya Allah…

Give me wisdom in my words.

Give me softness in my tone.

Let me respond with kindness — not ego.

Protect me from the need always to be right.

Protect my heart from taking questions personally.

Let my character speak when my knowledge falls short.

Let me be a source of light, not tension.

Ameen.

Heart Journal 12

What's the hardest question someone has asked you about your faith? How did it feel?

Write a few "go-to" responses that you can say with kindness and confidence.

How can you prepare your heart to respond with grace — even in difficult conversations?

Heart Journal 12

Heart Journal 12

CHAPTER 13

THE STRENGTH TO SAY NO — BOUNDARIES AS WORSHIP

There's a quiet kind of strength in being able to say, "No, I don't feel comfortable with that."

"No, I won't attend that gathering."

"No, I won't shake hands."

"No, I'm not going to compromise my faith."

And for many of us — especially as reverts — those words don't come easily.

We're taught to be agreeable, accommodating, and easygoing. When we enter Islam, we may carry the weight of wanting to please Allah and everyone around us.

But here's a truth worth repeating:

Saying "no" for the sake of Allah is an act of worship.

Boundaries are not rude. They are spiritual strength in action.

The Guilt That Creeps In

As a revert, it's common to feel torn between wanting to be accepted by family and friends and staying true to your deen.

You may say yes to things you're uncomfortable with to avoid conflict.

You may stay silent when someone crosses a line to keep the peace.

You may attend events that drain your soul, because you don't want to be the "difficult Muslim."

But Islam doesn't ask you to people-please.

It asks you to honor the boundaries Allah has set — and to honor yourself in the process.

Saying No with Dignity

You don't have to be aggressive or cold to set boundaries.

You can say no with softness, with wisdom, with grace. But say it.

Because every time you do, you send a message to your own soul:

My Islam matters. My peace matters. My connection with Allah matters.

Examples of gentle, firm boundaries:

"I'm grateful for the invite, but I won't be attending that event."

"That topic makes me uncomfortable — let's talk about something else."

"As a Muslim, I don't do that — I hope you understand."

"I know it might seem unusual, but this is part of my faith."

You don't owe anyone a debate. You owe Allah your sincerity.

When Boundaries Feel Lonely

Sometimes, the hardest part about saying no is the silence that follows.

People might pull away. Family might stop asking. Friends might misunderstand.

But Allah understands. And His closeness fills the gaps left by people who don't.

You might lose a few invitations — but you will gain barakah.

You might lose approval — but you will gain clarity.

You might lose comfort — but you will gain conviction.

And that is worth everything.

My Moment of Boundaries

I remember the first time I declined to shake a man's hand after embracing Islam.

It was at work, and it caught him off guard.

I felt my heart race. Although my voice was calm, inside, I was anxious. I explained briefly, kindly, that it was part of my faith.

He hesitated, then nodded. "I respect that," he said. And walked away.

That moment stayed with me — not because of how he reacted, but because of how I felt afterward.

Free. Firm. True to myself and my Rabb.

It was a small moment. But it was worship.

Boundaries Teach Others How to Respect You

You teach people to overlook your needs when you say yes to everything.

When you say no with sincerity, you teach them how to treat you with care.

Even if they don't understand your boundaries, they will come to respect the consistency, the dignity, and the peace you carry.

You don't need to prove your faith through discomfort.

You prove it through sincerity, balance, and courage to say, "I'm choosing Allah here."

The Prophet Muhammad ﷺ Had Boundaries Too

He ﷺ didn't say yes to every request. He prioritized certain people, limited his time, and gently corrected those who overstepped.

He showed us that rahmah (mercy) and limits are not opposites — they go hand in hand.

Your boundaries can also be a form of mercy—for yourself, your relationships, and your soul.

Heart Reflection: A Du'a for This Chapter

Ya Allah…

Give me the strength to say no when it protects my faith.

Let my boundaries be sincere, not prideful — peaceful, not harsh.

Help me stand firm when I'm misunderstood.

Replace any loss with closeness to You.

Help me set limits that nourish my heart and honor my deen.

And when I struggle, remind me that You are proud of every quiet act of sincerity.

Ameen.

Heart Journal 13

What boundaries have you struggled to set since becoming Muslim?

Write about a time you said "no" — or wish you had.

What kind of truthful phrases can you practice to protect your peace without guilt?

Heart Journal 13

Heart Journal 13

CHAPTER 14

FLOURISHING AT WORK, SCHOOL, AND PUBLIC LIFE

Being Muslim isn't something you only do in private. You carry it with you — in the break room, classrooms, business meetings, grocery store lines, airports.

And for reverts, that visibility can feel both empowering and uncomfortable.

You want to hold your head high — but sometimes you lower your gaze to avoid questions.

You want to pray on time — but you're not sure where.

You want to speak confidently — but you're afraid of being labeled, judged, or misunderstood.

Here's a reminder worth holding onto:

You were not meant to hide your light.

You were meant to walk with dignity — not just at home or at the masjid, but everywhere Allah places you.

You Belong in Every Space

Islam doesn't ask you to disappear from the world.

It asks you to show up with integrity, to work with excellence, to speak with wisdom, and to worship with devotion — no matter where you are.

You belong in professional settings.

You belong in academic spaces.

You belong in leadership.

You belong in creative fields.

You belong in service, science, art, education, entrepreneurship — all of it.

Not in spite of your Islam — but with your Islam.

The Awkward Conversations

Being a revert sometimes means fielding uncomfortable questions at work or school:

"So… are you fasting again?"

"Is it true Muslims can't…?"

"You're not allowed to celebrate birthdays?"

"Isn't that outfit hot in the summer?"

"Do you feel oppressed?"

At first, it can feel exhausting. But over time, these moments become easier. You'll find your rhythm, voice, and way of explaining things calmly, kindly, and confidently — or knowing when to let silence do the work.

You don't need to be defensive. You need to be grounded.

Visibility Is Da'wah

Your presence as a Muslim — your manners, your speech, your honesty, your excellence — is da'wah.

The way you stay respectful in disagreements. The way you show up early and work with care. The way you decline a party invite without being condescending.

All of it speaks.

Sometimes the most powerful da'wah is not what you say — but who you are.

And when people see your work ethic, your joy, your clarity — and then realize you're Muslim? That sticks.

You don't have to preach. Just be. Let your life speak.

A Moment at Work

I once politely refused a handshake from a man at work, and his surprise was immediate. I calmly explained that it was part of my religious practice.

He blinked, paused, and then said, "That's actually kind of respectable."

The moment passed. But it meant something.

Later, someone told me, "You made me think differently about Islam."

I didn't recite a hadith. I didn't hand out pamphlets.

I just stayed firm. Respectful. Consistent. And Allah did the rest.

Flourishing Doesn't Mean Fitting In

You don't have to blend in to succeed.

You don't need to mute your values to be accepted.

You don't have to compromise your deen to be respected.

Real flourishing is knowing who you are, no matter where you are.

And even if you're the only Muslim in the room — you are never alone.

Angels walk with you. Allah sees you. And your quiet courage is being written in your book of deeds.

Practical Tips for Public Confidence

Plan your prayer times: Know your break schedule. Ask respectfully if needed. Keep a small travel mat handy.

Pack food intentionally: Know what's halal, and bring your own if needed.

Have "go-to" explanations: Simple, kind ways to explain hijab, prayer, fasting, etc.

Dress confidently: Wear what reflects your values and makes you feel composed — even if it's different from those around you.

Set respectful boundaries: Decline what doesn't align with your beliefs, and do so with dignity.

You Represent — But You Don't Have to Be Perfect

It's true — many people will base their opinion of Islam on how you act.

That's a heavy thing to carry.

But remember: representation doesn't mean perfection.

If you make a mistake, own it. Apologize sincerely. Keep striving.

Don't carry the burden of being flawless — just be real, humble, and intentional.

Even the Prophet Muhammad ﷺ was reminded in the Qur'an that his job was to deliver, not to control hearts. Your job is to reflect light — not to force it.

Heart Reflection: A Du'a for This Chapter

Ya Allah…

Make me a reflection of Your mercy wherever I go.

Let my presence in public be a quiet form of da'wah.

Give me the confidence to pray, speak, and walk with my faith— even when I feel alone.

Protect me from the need for people.

Help me be consistent in worship, in character, and in courage.

Let my work be excellent, and my heart be at peace.

Ameen.

Heart Journal 14

Where do you feel most confident living your Islam in public? Where do you feel most unsure?

Describe a time you represented your faith in a way that surprised you — or others.

What's one thing you can start doing this week to flourish at work, school, or in public life with your faith, not despite it?

Heart Journal 14

PART III

FAITH IN ACTION — WORSHIP, DU'A, AND SPIRITUAL GROWTH

CHAPTER 15

SALAH THAT NOURISHES THE SOUL

In the beginning, salah can feel overwhelming.

You're learning words you don't fully understand.

You're trying to remember movements.

You're watching videos, asking questions, and repeating the same steps repeatedly.

You're afraid of "doing it wrong."

You feel rushed, distracted, or unsure if it's even working.

And yet — you keep showing up.

And that, right there, is where the nourishment begins.

Salah Is a Gift — Not a Test

Allah doesn't need our prayer.

We do.

We're not praying to prove our worth. We're praying to reconnect.

To realign.

To breathe again after the noise of the day.

Even when your recitation is choppy, your mind wanders, and your prayer feels less like a connection and more like a checklist — it still counts.

It's still seen.

It's still honored.

Because the fact that you stopped the world to face your Lord — even in imperfect form — *is a miracle.*

The Day I Prayed and Felt It

There was a moment — months after I took shahada — when I prayed not because I had to… but because I wanted to.

It was quiet. Simple. Nothing special from the outside.

But in sujood, I lingered.

And something softened inside me.

I didn't know all the Arabic. I didn't have tears running down my face. But I felt something settle — like I had finally exhaled.

And I thought, So this is what people mean when they say salah is a conversation.

I remembered the words of Shaykh Yaser Birjas: *'Savor the sweetness of salah.'*

Not just pray it — but truly taste it. Let it melt into your heart, slowly and intentionally, like something precious you don't want to rush."

I felt light — as if something invisible had been lifted off me. I felt calm — like the heart had finally exhaled.

That moment stayed with me.

It reminded me that salah wasn't just an obligation but a mercy. A lifeline.

From Ritual to Relationship

The shift happens slowly:

At first, you pray because you're told to.

Then you pray because you're afraid not to.

Then you pray because you're learning discipline.

And eventually… you pray because you miss it.

That's when salah moves from ritual to relationship.

Not every prayer will be spiritual. Some days, it will still feel rushed or mechanical. But over time, your heart begins to crave that stillness—the grounding—the moment of placing your forehead on the earth and remembering your origin—and your return.

The Little Things That Deepen Salah

If you want your prayer to feel more nourishing, start with small shifts:

Pray on time, even if briefly — it protects the rhythm of your day.

Memorize the meaning of what you're saying — even one phrase at a time.

Slow down — even if you only pray two rak'ahs, give them your full presence.

Make du'a in your own language before or after prayer.

Imagine Allah is watching you lovingly — not harshly — because He is.

These shifts aren't dramatic. But over time, they change how you pray.

And how you live.

When It's Hard to Pray

Let's be honest: some days, you won't feel like praying.

You'll feel emotionally distant.

Or mentally overwhelmed.

Or spiritually numb.

Or simply tired.

That doesn't make you a hypocrite.

It makes you human.

And here's the incredible part: even the prayer you struggle to pray is accepted — sometimes more so than the prayer that felt easy.

The Prophet Muhammad ﷺ taught us that effort is honored. That persistence is loved by Allah.

So, if you pray while feeling disconnected — that is still worship.

And if you miss a prayer, but return with remorse — that return is beautiful to your Lord.

Your Prayer Is Always Worth It

You are not too late.

You are not too behind.

You are not too broken to build a meaningful relationship with Salah.

Prayer is not just for the pious. It's what makes us righteous.

So, keep showing up.

Even when it feels dry.

Even when you're doubting.

Even when it's the only thing you're holding onto.

Because one day — one sujood — will feel like coming home.

And your heart will say: Alhamdulillah, I kept praying.

Heart Reflection: A Du'a for This Chapter

Ya Allah…

Let me fall in love with Salah.

Let it be a place of peace, not pressure.

Let it nourish my heart, calm my mind, and remind me that I'm never alone.

Forgive me for the prayers I've missed.

Accept the ones I've rushed.

And reward the ones I struggled to complete.

Let me never walk away from Your presence — even when I'm tired.

Let my sujood be a place of safety, healing, and return.

Ameen.

"Truly it is in the remembrance of Allah that hearts find rest."

— Surah Ar-Ra'd 13:28

Heart Journal 15

Describe a time you prayed and felt spiritually full — even briefly. What made that moment different?

What emotions or memories are tied to Salah for you?

What's one small change you can make to bring more presence or love into your prayer this week?

Heart Journal 15

Heart Journal 15

CHAPTER 16

DU'A THAT FEELS PERSONAL

There's a special kind of silence that follows a sincere du'a. A stillness in your heart. A softness in your breath. A weight released — even if the answer hasn't come yet.

Du'a is not just a ritual.

It's not just Arabic words or memorized phrases.

It's the pouring out of your soul to the One who already knows everything — and still wants to hear from you.

And once you begin to experience it that way, du'a no longer feels distant.

It feels personal. Intimate. Healing.

Talk to Allah Like You Know He's Listening

You don't need perfect words.

You don't need fancy Islamic terms.

You don't even need to raise your hands — though you can.

What you need is sincerity.

Because what Allah looks at is your heart, not your eloquence.

And sometimes, the most powerful du'a is the one made in stammered whispers between sobs. Or the one made without words at all — just a deep sigh, a hopeful glance, or a single tear.

The Prophet Muhammad ﷺ said:

"Du'a is worship."

(Tirmidhi)

That means every time you turn to Allah — with joy, with sorrow, with longing — you are worshiping.

When Du'a Feels Distant

There are seasons when you struggle to even raise your hands.

You wonder, What's the point?

You question whether your words matter.

You feel like nothing is changing, or maybe you feel too broken to even begin.

I've been there.

And what I learned is this: even the decision to try and make du'a is an act of turning toward Allah.

Even if your words feel hollow.

Even if your voice cracks.

Even if you must start with, "Ya Allah, I don't even know what to say."

He hears you.

Speaking to Allah in the Language of Your Soul

There is no barrier between you and Allah — not even language.

Your du'a doesn't need to be in Arabic to be heard. It doesn't need eloquence to be accepted. It only needs to be real.

Speak to Him in the language your soul understands — the one you think in, cry in, dream in. Whether that's English, Urdu, French or Spanish — He understands. He always has.

You can whisper to Him while driving for an errand. Pour your heart out while watching the sunset. Let your tears fall without words at all — and He will still know exactly what you meant.

Some of the sincerest du'as are the ones no one else will ever hear — the quiet pleadings made on long drives, the silent hopes buried in a pillow, the scribbled prayers in an old notebook.

These are not small. These are not forgotten. These are the sacred conversations between you and the One who listens without judgment and responds with love.

My Du'a Moments

Some of my most personal du'as weren't planned. They came in waves. In the middle of the night. During sujood. Or while folding laundry.

One of them came after heartbreak — when I said, "Ya Allah, I don't know what's good for me anymore. But You do. Please choose for me."

Another came after I felt like a failure — when I whispered, "Ya Allah, please don't let this be the end of my story."

Years later, I look back and realize: those prayers were answered. Just not in the way I imagined. In a better way.

Du'a Is a Lifeline, Not a Last Resort

Sometimes we treat du'a like the last thing we try — after we've exhausted everything else.

But du'a is meant to be our first response, not our backup plan.

It's not weakness — it's wisdom. It's surrender. It's strength in its purest form.

When you say, "Ya Allah, help me," — you're not giving up. You're tapping into the One who never fails.

And when nothing else makes sense, du'a does.

Tips for a More Personal Du'a Life

Start with gratitude: "Ya Allah, thank You for…"

Name your feelings: "I feel scared, confused, tired…"

Ask specifically: Not just for "ease," but what kind of ease you need

Be honest: Even if what you're asking for feels small, messy, or selfish — tell Him anyway

Make du'a when things are good, not just when you're desperate — show up for the relationship

What If I Don't Get What I Asked For?

It's one of the hardest truths in du'a: sometimes the answer is not yet, not this, or something better.

And it can hurt.

But Allah promises — no du'a goes unanswered. It is:

Given immediately

Delayed for a better time

Replaced with something better

Or held as reward in the Hereafter

Your words are never wasted.

Your tears are never ignored.

Your du'a is always recorded — even if the response is silent for now.

Heart Reflection: A Du'a for This Chapter

Ya Allah…

Let me come to You without fear.

Let my du'a be raw, honest, and full of trust.

Hear the things I'm too shy to say out loud.

Heal the wounds I keep trying to hide.

When I feel distant, pull me nearby.

When I don't know what to ask for, just give me what I need.

Make me someone who speaks to You easily — like a friend, like a servant, like someone who knows You care.

And when I can't speak at all —

listen to the silence and answer me with Your mercy.

Ameen.

"He knows what is within the hearts."

— Surah Al-Mulk 67:13

Heart Journal 16

Write a du'a that reflects where you are right now — without editing yourself.

What's something you've asked Allah for, and how did He answer it (even if it wasn't in the way you expected)?

What would your du'a sound like if you knew — without a doubt — that Allah was listening with love?

Heart Journal 16

Heart Journal 16

CHAPTER 17

ISTIKARAH AND THE POWER OF TRUSTING ALLAH

When you first learn about istikharah, it sounds like a secret door to certainty.

A special prayer. A direct line to divine clarity. A way to make the "right" choice, especially when you're unsure.

And that's not far from the truth — but istikharah isn't about getting a magical yes or no. It's about trust.

It's about handing your heart to Allah and saying:

"If this is good for me, bring it closer.

If it's not, take it away.

And make me content either way."

What Istikharah Really Is

The Prophet Muhammad ﷺ used to teach the Companions the du'a of istikhrah the way he taught a surah of the Qur'an — that's how important it was.

It's not a formula. It's not reserved for scholars. It's not just for marriage.

It's a powerful tool for any major decision:

Moving to a new city

Taking a job offer

Starting school

Entering or leaving a relationship

Making a big purchase

Saying yes to something that feels risky

Istikharah is saying:

Ya Allah, I trust You more than I trust myself.

What to Expect After Istikharah

One of the biggest misconceptions is that you'll get a sign — a clear dream or a specific feeling.

But often, istikharah shows up through:

A door closing

A sense of unease

A delay or obstacle you hadn't anticipated

Or, on the flip side, a path that suddenly feels smoother, supported, and peaceful

It's not about getting what you want.

It's about being guided toward what's best — even when you don't understand it yet.

Trusting What You Can't See

As reverts, many of us have had to make huge life decisions — without much guidance.

We may not have family to consult. We may not have community support. We may feel unsure if we're "doing it right."

But here's the beauty of istikharah:

It removes the burden of figuring everything out on your own.

It hands the decision to the One who sees the full picture.

Even if you don't know where the road is leading — you can trust that He does.

How to Pray Istikharah (Quick Refresher)

Pray two rak'ahs of voluntary prayer (any time that's not forbidden).

After you finish, recite the du'a of istikharah (in Arabic or translation if needed).

Then go about your decision — observe how things unfold.

If you're still unsure, repeat the du'a over the next few days.

You don't have to wait passively. Do your research. Ask trusted friends. Make your effort.

But let your heart lean on Allah.

My Relationship with Istikharah

I can't count how many times I've made istikharah.

When I was confused. When I had a strong desire but needed to check my heart.

When I didn't trust my own judgment.

Sometimes, I'd feel a sudden clarity — a kind of deep calm that settled the restlessness.

Other times, the path I wanted would quietly fall away.

And I'd whisper, "Ya Allah, thank You for protecting me — even when I didn't see it."

Istikharah became more than a du'a.

It became a habit of trust.

A way to remind myself: I don't know what's best. But You do.

It's Okay to Be Unsure

Making istikharah doesn't guarantee instant answers.

You might still wrestle with confusion.

You might still go back and forth.

That's not a sign of failure — it's a sign of sincerity.

Because istikharah isn't just about the outcome.

It's about the process of submission.

It's saying, "I want what You want for me — even if it's not what I expected."

And that kind of trust changes everything.

What If I Still Make the "Wrong" Choice?

That's one of the biggest fears people carry.

But when you've genuinely turned to Allah, and done your part with du'a and effort —

then even the detours are part of the journey.

Sometimes Allah lets you walk down a road that doesn't last —

not to punish you, but to teach you.

And sometimes, the heartbreak was the answer to your du'a —

a mercy wrapped in difficulty.

Trust: when you ask Allah to guide you,

He will.

Even if it looks different than what you imagined.

You Won't Always Feel Confident — But You Can Feel Content

You may never feel 100% sure. That's okay.

Certainty isn't always a feeling — sometimes it's a decision to trust.

And when you trust Allah's plan over your own, you can move forward — even into the unknown — with a quiet kind of confidence.

Because if it's written for you, nothing can take it away.

And if it's not… you don't want it, no matter how beautiful it seemed.

A Note for the Hard "No"

Sometimes, what we wanted most is what Allah gently removes.

And it hurts.

You wonder, Why show it to me at all? Why let me get attached?

But what if the very thing that's breaking your heart… is the thing that would have broken your spirit had you held onto it?

Allah is not cruel. He is Al-Hakim — **The Most Wise.**

And when He closes a door, He holds your hand until you're strong enough to walk toward something better.

Heart Reflection: A Du'a for This Chapter

Ya Allah…

Guide my heart when I don't know which way to go.

Make the right path easy, and the wrong path hard to reach.

Protect me from decisions made in haste.

Help me wait without worry.

Let me feel peace, even when the answer is "no."

Ya Allah, I trust You more than I trust myself.

Choose for me — and make me love what You've chosen.

Ameen.

Heart Journal 17

Write about a time you had to make a big decision. How did you feel before and after?

What would it look like for you to truly trust Allah's plan — even if it's not the one you imagined?

What would it be if you could ask Allah for guidance on one decision right now?

Heart Journal 17

Heart Journal 17

CHAPTER 18
CREATING A PERSONAL IBADAH RHYTHM

It's easy to fall into extremes.

You either want to do everything — wake up for tahajjud, memorize Qur'an, fast Mondays and Thursdays, attend every class…

Or you feel overwhelmed and do nothing, afraid that whatever you manage just won't be enough.

But here's a gentle truth:

Allah does not expect perfection — He invites consistency.

And that's where your personal ibadah rhythm comes in.

It's not about checking boxes.

It's not about copying someone else's schedule.

It's about building a rhythm of worship that suits your life, energy, and season.

Ibadah Is Meant to Fit Into Your Life — Not Crush It

Sometimes we think that being religious means squeezing our lives around rituals. But the beauty of Islam is that worship weaves through your day.

Cooking becomes ibadah when you say Bismillah.

Resting becomes ibadah when you do it with intention.

Working becomes ibadah when done with honesty.

Caring for children or parents becomes ibadah when done with patience.

Saying SubhanAllah while walking becomes ibadah.

You don't need to do more.

You need to do things with more presence — and let that presence guide you back to Allah.

Start Where You Are — Not Where You Wish You Were

Maybe you want to be someone who prays tahajjud — but right now, you're struggling to pray on time.

Maybe you want to memorize Qur'an — but haven't opened a mushaf in weeks.

Maybe you want to fast regularly — but your mental health or physical state doesn't allow it right now.

That's okay.

The most powerful ibadah is the kind that's realistic and sincere.

Start with:

One du'a in the morning

One quiet moment after salah

One small surah revisited each day

One act of kindness done for Allah's sake

And build from there — slowly, intentionally, joyfully.

Your Rhythm Can Change With Your Life

What works in one season may not work in another.

A mother of young children might not have quiet time for long salah, but her patience and service are beloved acts of worship.

A busy student might not attend every halaqah, but reviewing Qur'an between classes counts.

A working professional may not have energy for extras, but making du'a during the commute still carries weight.

Allah sees your effort. He knows your circumstances. He never asks more than you can give.

And sometimes, the most spiritual thing you can do… is rest.

My Ibadah in Different Seasons

There was a time I woke up regularly for tahajjud. My soul craved it, and my schedule allowed it. I felt nourished.

And then life shifted — new responsibilities, emotional fatigue, changing routines.

I couldn't do everything I used to. At first, I felt guilty. But then I remembered: Allah doesn't measure me by what I used to do — He rewards me for what I try to do now.

So I found a new rhythm: shorter du'as, slower recitations, quick dhikr while washing dishes, and a moment of stillness before bed.

And it was enough.

Let Ibadah Fill Your Day — Not Just Your Planner

It's okay if your acts of worship are quiet and hidden.

It's okay if you don't post about them.

It's okay if no one else sees how you choose Allah daily.

Because He sees.

And when you begin to weave ibadah into the ordinary — your life begins to feel extraordinary.

Building Your Ibadah Rhythm: A Gentle Guide

1. Anchor your day with salah.

Make prayer the spine of your schedule, not the afterthought.

2. Choose 1–2 small extras.

Maybe it's a daily dhikr. A weekly fast. A weekly charity. Keep it light.

3. Reflect regularly.

Ask yourself: What's helping me connect? What's making me feel burned out?

4. Make space for joy.

Let your ibadah feel uplifting, not draining. Use candles, scents, spray perfume on your prayer dress, and create a peaceful corner to celebrate your worship.

5. Adjust as needed.

Your rhythm is not a contract. It's a living relationship. Let it evolve.

Heart Reflection: A Du'a for This Chapter

Ya Allah…

Help me create a rhythm of worship that nourishes my soul.

Let me do what I can — with love, not guilt.

Remind me that You see even the smallest acts done with sincerity.

Let my days be filled with Your remembrance, even in the quietest ways.

And if I fall out of rhythm, bring me back — gently, and with hope.

Ameen.

Heart Journal 18

What acts of worship feel most nourishing to you right now?

What's one small ibadah habit you can commit to this week — and why?

Write a "schedule of the soul" — not by the hour, but by moments of meaning you want to build into your day.

Heart Journal 18

Heart Journal 18

CHAPTER 19

RECONNECTING WITH THE QUR'AN IN YOUR OWN WAY

You want to love the Qur'an.

You know it's the most sacred book.

You know it's the literal word of Allah.

You know it's a guide, a mercy, a light.

But still… sometimes it feels distant.

Maybe you've tried reading it cover to cover.

You may have started a memorization plan but got overwhelmed.

Maybe you don't understand Arabic and worry you're "doing it wrong."

Maybe you only open it when you're in pain — and then feel guilty for neglecting it the rest of the time.

If this is you, you're not alone.

And here's your reminder: You can reconnect with the Qur'an in your own way — and in your own time.

It's Not About Perfection — It's About Presence

The Qur'an wasn't revealed to overwhelm you.

It was revealed to transform you.

To reach your heart. To guide your steps. To remind you that you are never, ever alone.

Even if you read and reflect on one ayah deeply — that's a relationship.

Even if you listen to a recitation during your commute and feel peace — that's connection.

Even if you cry over a translation that finally speaks to your situation — that's intimacy.

The Qur'an meets you where you are.

And then — gently — it begins to lift you higher.

Your First Qur'an Might've Felt Like a Textbook

When you first embraced Islam, you may have bought all the "big" books:

Sahih al-Bukhari. Riyad-us-Saliheen. A thick Qur'an with transliteration.

I remember browsing bookstores in Devon Street in Chicago, arms full of texts that made me feel scholarly and excited.

But I didn't know where to begin.

I read here and there. I highlighted. But mostly… those books sat on the shelf.

Visible reminders that I was Muslim — but I still didn't feel connected yet.

And that's okay.

Sometimes, the presence of the Qur'an in your life precedes the relationship.

Sometimes, it takes time for the words to sink from the page into your heart.

When the Qur'an Starts Speaking to You

There comes a moment — maybe during salah, maybe in a late-night scroll, maybe during grief — when an ayah hits different.

You read it and feel like it was written just for you.

"So truly where there is hardship, there is also ease."

(Surah Ash-Sharh 94:6)

"And He is with you wherever you are."

(Surah Al-Hadid 57:4)

"Call upon Me; I will respond to you."

(Surah Ghafir 40:60)

And suddenly… the Qur'an stops feeling like something "out there."

It feels like it's yours.

A conversation. A mirror. A mercy.

That's the moment everything changes.

But Am I Allowed to Read It This Way?

Some reverts worry:

"Is it wrong to emotionally interpret the Qur'an before I understand Arabic?"

"Can I feel moved by a translation, or is that not valid?"

Here's the truth: your emotional connection is a gift — not a flaw.

No, not every ayah can be interpreted through feelings alone.

Yes, Arabic holds depth that translations can't fully carry.

But your heart being moved is not bid'ah. It's barakah.

It means your soul is responding to the Light.

And Allah knows your intention. He knows you're drawing near. He knows you want to love His words.

So don't be afraid to feel the Qur'an, even as you keep learning to understand it better.

My Love for Surah Ar-Rahman

There was a time in my life when I felt completely unworthy of Allah's mercy.

I was grieving, questioning everything, and unsure how to move forward.

And then I listened to Surah Ar-Rahman.

"Then which of the favors of your Lord will you deny?"

The repetition washed over me. Again, and again.

I wasn't sure if I was "allowed" to read it that way — like a personal message.

But it felt like it was written just for my wounds. And I cried.

To this day, that surah brings me home to myself.

It reminds me that mercy is always there — even when I'm not sure I deserve it.

Ways to Reconnect Gently with the Qur'an

Choose one ayah a day.

Just one. Sit with it. Reflect. Journal. Carry it with you.

Listen to recitation while doing everyday things.

Let it flow into your life — cooking, commuting, winding down.

Pair reading with a trusted translation.

Understand what you're reading, even in pieces.

Let your emotions be part of the process.

Joy, grief, awe — it all belongs.

Make du'a before you open it.

"Ya Allah, let me hear what I need. Let me feel closer to You."

You Don't Have to Finish It — Just Keep Coming Back

You may never read the Qur'an cover to cover.

You may read the same surahs over and over again.

You may memorize slowly, forget, then relearn.

That's okay.

The point isn't to "complete" the Qur'an.

It's to let it complete you.

To let it shape how you see yourself.

How you speak. How you forgive. How you trust.

How you keep going — even when life feels too hard.

Heart Reflection: A Du'a for This Chapter

Ya Allah…

Let the Qur'an become my companion.

Let its words live in my heart, not just my hands.

Make me love it — not just read it.

Make me feel it — not just recite it.

Let me find myself in its verses.

Let me heal through its mercy.

And let it be a light for me in this life and the next.

Ameen.

Heart Journal 19

What is your current relationship with the Qur'an? How do you feel about it?

Write about a time an ayah struck you in a personal way. Why do you think it touched you?

What's one small way you can reconnect with the Qur'an this week — without pressure?

Heart Journal 19

Heart Journal 19

CHAPTER 20

LOVING THE PROPHET MUHAMMAD  WITHOUT FEELING UNWORTHY

When you first enter Islam, you know that loving the Prophet Muhammad ﷺ is part of the faith.

You say his name with reverence.

You hear stories of his character.

You see Muslims around the world weep at the mention of him — calling him Habibi, sending Salawat, longing to visit Madinah.

And yet… sometimes, you feel a little behind.

Maybe you don't feel that deep connection yet.

Maybe you wonder, "Do I love him enough?"

Maybe you feel unworthy of his legacy.

If that's you — breathe.

Because loving the Prophet Muhammad ﷺ is not about perfection.

It's about sincerity. And the door is always open.

A Distant History… or a Living Example?

When you're a revert, the Prophet Muhammad ﷺ can feel distant at first.

He lived in 7th-century Arabia, spoke a language you may not know, and was accompanied by giants of the faith. His world felt far from yours.

But here's what bridges that gap: his mercy, humanity, and heart.

He wasn't just a figure in a book.

He was someone who comforted the grieving.

Who cried when people suffered.

Who stood up for the oppressed.

Who joked with children.

Who forgave people who harmed him.

Who prayed for you — yes, you — before you were even born.

"I wish I could see my brothers," he said.

The companions asked, "Are we not your brothers?"

He replied, "You are my companions. My brothers are those who believe in me without having seen me.

(Muslim)

That's you.

He was thinking of you.

You Don't Have to Be Perfect to Love Him

Sometimes we think we must "fix ourselves" before we can claim to love the Prophet Muhammad ﷺ.

We imagine that only those who follow every sunnah, dress perfectly, and never miss a prayer are worthy of that love.

But love often comes before perfection.

Think of how many people in his life were still learning, still struggling — and he ﷺ still loved them.

The Bedouin who urinated in the masjid

The woman who committed a major sin but repented

The companions who fell into mistakes and returned again and again

He never rejected someone who came to him sincerely.

So don't disqualify yourself.

Come as you are. He ﷺ would have welcomed you.

A Personal Realization

For a long time, I respected the Prophet ﷺ but didn't feel emotionally close to him. I saw him as a noble figure but not someone I had a relationship with.

Then I read a story about him ﷺ standing for a funeral — and when he was told it was a non-Muslim's body, he replied, "Was he not a human soul?"

Sahih al-Bukhari, Hadith 1312

This narration is used to illustrate the Prophet Muhammad's ﷺ respect for human dignity, regardless of religious affiliation. His response, *"Was he not a soul?"*, emphasizes the sanctity of all human life.

That moment pierced me. His heart was wide, compassionate, and aware of human dignity—regardless of labels.

And I thought… If this is who he was, then I want to be near him, learn from him, and love him."

It wasn't instant. But it started something.

Now, when I say Allahumma salli 'ala Muhammad, I don't just say it with my lips — I say it with my heart.

Small Ways to Build Love for the Prophet Muhammad ﷺ

You don't need to force a feeling. Just nurture it, like a seed:

Read one story about his character each week.

Send salawat (blessings) upon him daily — even quietly.

Picture him making du'a for you.

Reflect on how he treated the most vulnerable.

Practice one sunnah (even smiling!) with the intention of nearness.

Visit Madinah if you can and speak to him with your heart.

Love grows through time, remembrance, and sincerity — not shame.

He Prayed for You Through Your Pain

One of the most comforting hadiths is this:

"My ummah, my ummah…"

These were the words the Prophet Muhammad ﷺ kept repeating when he was worried on the Day of Judgment.

Even in his final moments, his concern was for us.

Not just the sahabah. Not just scholars. Us.

You, the Muslim who's still figuring things out.

You, the one who converted with more questions than answers.

You, the one who feels like you're always behind.

He loved you before you ever knew his name.

You Don't Have to Be Arab, or Born Muslim, or "Relatable"

He ﷺ welcomed people from every tribe, status, and background.

You don't need to come from a Muslim family to belong to his ummah.

You don't need to pronounce Arabic perfectly to be heard.

You don't need to have your life all figured out to be loved.

You already belong.

And your love — even if imperfect — is valuable.

When Shame Blocks the Heart

It's common to feel like, "If the Prophet Muhammad ﷺ saw me right now, he'd be disappointed."

But remember he ﷺ was sent as a mercy, not a burden.

He would see your tears and pray for you.

He would hear your du'a and say Ameen.

He would see your mistakes and invite you back to Allah — not with judgment but hope.

Let your shame turn into motivation. Let it soften you. Let it open the door to love — not close it.

Heart Reflection: A Du'a for This Chapter

Ya Allah…

Let me love the Prophet Muhammad ﷺ not just in words, but in action.

Let me feel close to him — even across time, even through imperfection.

Let his compassion be a mirror for my own.

Let his mercy awaken mine.

Let me be among those he called "my brothers and sisters."

And when I fall short, let my longing be enough to draw me near.

Ameen.

Heart Journal 20

What are your earliest impressions of the Prophet Muhammad ﷺ? How have they changed?

What's one story about his life that resonates with your heart — and why?

Write a letter to him — what would you want him to know about your journey?

WHAT IS HAYA? HAYA AS A SHIELD IN MODERN LIFE

Before Islam, I thought modesty was just about clothing. Long skirts. Covered hair. Not attracting attention.

But when I came into this faith, I learned that *haya* is so much deeper than fabric. It's a condition of the heart — a softness, a shyness, a reverent humility before Allah.

Haya is what makes you lower your gaze not just from others, but from sin. It's what makes you pause before replying in anger. It's what keeps you from overexposing your life online, even when everyone else is oversharing. It's what teaches you to ask: *"Would I want Allah to see me like this?"* — and then act accordingly.

I remember once being invited to a relative's casual backyard gathering. Before Islam, this would've been easy — jeans, a tank top, blending right in. But now I hesitated. I wore my long dress, my hijab, and told myself, "Just be kind and be yourself."

A man at the party tried to approach me with a flirtatious comment. I smiled politely, lowered my gaze, and turned back toward the women's circle. One of the other guests later came up and said, "You handled that with so much class… I don't know what it is about you, but it's peaceful."

That was *haya*. Not hiding — but protecting.

Another time, I was on a work trip. A colleague invited me out for drinks after the conference. I politely declined and said, "I don't do that anymore. I'm Muslim." She didn't press. But later, another co-worker came to me and said, "I've been wanting to stop drinking, too. Seeing you set that boundary without guilt made me think — maybe I can also change."

That's the quiet ripple of *haya*. It doesn't preach. It just lives in truth — and others feel it.

Even in the digital world, haya saves me. There are posts I want to make… photos I almost share… But something pulls me back. Not shame. Not fear. Just a whisper that says, *"Not everything needs to be public."*

Sometimes, *haya* is deleting the text before you send it. Sometimes, it's staying silent when your ego wants to argue. Sometimes, it's dressing with intention even when you're just going to the grocery store.

To some, it might look like I'm holding back. But to me, it feels like I'm being held — by something greater.

Haya isn't weakness. It's strength wrapped in grace. It's Allah giving you a filter for your soul, so you don't have to walk unguarded in a noisy, tempting world.

And the more I learn to embody it, the freer I feel.

Heart Reflection: The Gift of Haya

Reflect on a moment when you felt protected by your modesty — in speech, dress, or presence. What might have happened if you hadn't had that boundary?

In what areas of your life would you like to practice more *ḥaya*?

What does modesty look like for you — beyond clothing?

A Du'a for Haya

Ya Allah, Let modesty dwell in my heart, So that my words, my steps, my silence, and my presence are all guarded by You.

Make haya a shield for my soul in a world that tempts me to forget who I am. Beautify me with inner dignity. Let others feel peace around me — not because of what I say, but because of how I carry the light of You.

Ameen.

Heart Journal 21

When was a time you felt protected by your modesty — whether in speech, dress, or presence? Reflect on how that moment unfolded. What would have been different if you didn't have haya guiding you?

Heart Journal 21

Heart Journal 21

CHAPTER 22

CULTIVATING KHUSHU IN SALAH

There is a kind of strength that isn't loud. It doesn't come from public recognition or perfect routines. It's the kind of strength that is built slowly, in secret. Like the stillness of your heart when it bows in prayer.

That strength is called *khushu* — A presence. A softening. A sacred focus that draws you into closeness with your Lord.

But khushu doesn't always arrive easily. Sometimes your mind is busy. Sometimes your heart feels numb. Sometimes you go through the motions, whispering Arabic words without feeling their weight.

And truthfully — there are still so many times I forget. I forget how many rakah I've prayed. I wonder: Did I say the tashahhud? Did I repeat a surah twice by mistake? Did I miss something important?

And in those moments, my heart quietly says: **"Ya Allah, forgive me. You know I'm trying."**

That's what keeps me grounded — not getting every motion right, but turning back to Allah with humility and hope.

Khushu grows in the soil of sincerity, not perfection. It deepens with practice, with du'a, with effort that no one else sees.

If you want to feel more present in your salah, try starting with the smallest of intentions:

- Whisper *Allahu Akbar* like you're truly leaving the world behind.
- Pause after Al-Fatiha and let its meanings soak into your heart.
- Choose a short surah that moves you — even if you've heard it a hundred times.
- Slow your pace. Let each bow, each prostration, be a meeting — not a routine.

And most importantly, **speak to Allah like He's listening.** Because He is.

There's no secret formula to perfect khushu. But there is sincerity. And Allah loves sincerity more than performance.

Even if you drift in salah, keep returning. Even if you feel far, keep showing up. Every time you come back, you're planting a seed. And one day, you may find yourself in sujood, and realize your heart never wants to leave.

That's what khushu feels like.

Not perfection. But presence. And peace.

A Du'a for When You Want to Feel Salah Again

Ya Allah, Sometimes I forget. Sometimes I rush. Sometimes I stand before You, and my heart feels distant — lost in worries, tangled in dunya.

But I still come. And I still want You.

Let my salah be more than movement. Let it be a meeting with You. Let me whisper Allahu Akbar and truly mean that nothing is greater than You.

When I forget how many rakah I've prayed, when I stumble through words I'm still learning, forgive me — and accept me.

Plant khushu in my heart like a seed that grows with every sujood. Make me crave prayer the way I crave peace. And let me one day weep, not out of guilt — but out of closeness to You.

Ameen.

Heart Journal 22

What moments during prayer feel the most distracted for you? And when have you felt even a flicker of connection — even if it was brief, even if it surprised you?

What would help your heart be more present next time? A slower pace? A favorite surah? A quiet room?

You are not failing. You are learning intimacy with your Lord — one breath at a time.

Heart Journal 22

PART IV

RELATIONSHIPS, FAMILY, AND QUIET IMPACT

CHAPTER 23

WHEN BARAKAH IS BETTER THAN BEAUTY

When people talk about choosing a spouse, they often list what sounds good on paper: Successful. Handsome. Financially stable. Educated.

But Islam teaches us something deeper. The Prophet Muhammad ﷺ said:

"A woman is married for four things: her wealth, her family status, her beauty and her religion. So you should marry the religious woman, [otherwise] you will be a loser." (Bukhari and Muslim)

This guidance doesn't just apply to men choosing women — it applies to all of us.

Sometimes, the heart is drawn to what sparkles — the wealth, the looks, the accolades. But the soul… the soul longs for something deeper. A man who prays in the quiet of the night. A woman whose tongue remembers Allah more than the world. A home built on du'a, not display.

Marriage in Islam isn't about crafting a perfect picture for others. It's about choosing a companion who helps you reach Jannah. Someone whose character anchors you when your emotions waver. Someone who reminds you of your Lord when you forget.

You may be offered many things. But not all gifts come with barakah. Not all beauty brings peace.

Barakah shows up in the way you feel safe speaking your fears. In shared sujood. In the way the house feels light, even if it's small. In laughter that isn't loud, but sincere.

Sometimes, the person who looks ideal on paper may not be the one who sees your soul in sujood. And sometimes, the one who walks with quiet dignity, who listens more than he speaks, who prays gently beside his mother — he's the one who will carry your du'as like his own.

Barakah doesn't always look impressive to others. It may come wrapped in simplicity — in someone who doesn't speak fluent Arabic but loves the Qur'an deeply. Someone who isn't wealthy, but whose presence feels like provision.

If you're in the season of choosing, don't just ask: *"Are they everything I dreamed of?"* Ask instead: *"Will they help me grow closer to Allah?"*

Because beauty fades. Careers shift. Looks change. But the one who brings barakah — brings light. And light lingers long after the sparkle fades.

Barakah is found in a shared plate of rice. In one blanket and two hearts that make du'a for the same tomorrow. In love that is patient, prayerful, and full of *tawakkul.*

So don't chase what dazzles. Choose what is steady. What is sincere. What is blessed.

Marriage, in the end, is not about the wedding. It's not about the pictures, or the gifts, or the story you tell others. It's about who stands beside you when no one is looking. It's about finding someone who makes you more you — the *you* that pleases Allah.

The Prophet Muhammad ﷺ said:

"The best marriage is the one with the least burden."

And I believe that. Sometimes, that kind of love only comes after loss. After divorce. After heartbreak. After lessons learned in the shadows.

But oh, when it comes… It tastes like mercy.

A Du'a for Choosing Well

Ya Allah, *Let my heart choose what brings me closer to You — not the flashiest option, but the one with the deepest barakah.*

Grant me a spouse who honors the Qur'an, who walks with humility, who gives without asking for return.

And if I've already found them — let me never forget the gift that they are.

Let our marriage be a mercy, a mirror, a means to Jannah.

Because I don't want to be perfect. I want barakah. The kind that lingers in silence, grows in struggle, and stays — long after beauty fades.

Ameen.

Heart Journal 23

What qualities do you truly value in a life partner — beyond appearances and status?

Can you recall a moment when you were tested to choose between the easy path and the path of faith?

How have your relationships — past or present — drawn you closer to Allah?

Heart Journal 23

CHAPTER 24

WHEN FRIENDS DON'T UNDERSTAND YOUR FAITH

You thought they'd be happy for you.

Maybe not fully on board — but at least supportive.

After all, they knew your heart. You shared secrets, laughter, years of life together.

So when you told them you embraced Islam,

you braced for awkwardness…

but you didn't expect silence.

Or confusion.

Or distance.

Or side-eyes.

Or subtle comments like:

"So, you don't celebrate birthdays anymore?"

"You're not allowed to have fun now?"

"This is just a phase, right?"

And suddenly, the people who once felt like home… feel like strangers.

This Is One of the Quiet Losses of Reversion

No one warns you about this.

About the grief that comes not from a big dramatic fallout —

but from the slow fading of friendships that once mattered.

You still love them.

You still care.

But now your life orbits around something they don't understand.

And that difference — if left unspoken — becomes a wall.

This doesn't make you weak.

It makes you human.

We were created for connection — and losing it hurts.

It's Not Always About Malice

Sometimes, your friends aren't being cruel. They just don't know how to process the change.

They might feel replaced.

They might feel like you're judging them (even when you're not).

They might be uncomfortable with their own beliefs now that you've chosen a clear path.

Or they might simply not know what to say.

Reversion to Islam is a deep transformation — and not everyone is ready to witness it up close.

And that's okay.

It doesn't make your journey less valid.

It just means your path is different now — and that difference may take time to navigate.

The Questions That Cut

Sometimes, it's not the silence that hurts — it's the offhand remarks.

"Are you even the same person anymore?"

"So you think you're better now?"

"Why would you follow that religion?"

"Do you even drink coffee with us anymore?"

"What happened to the old you?"

You may laugh it off.

Or try to explain.

Or walk away with a heavy heart.

Know this: every time you choose Allah over approval; you are being strengthened — even if it stings.

What If They Never Come Around?

That's one of the hardest realities.

Some friends may pull away completely.

Some may stop calling.

Some may reappear only to argue or "save" you.

You can't control how they react.

But you can control how you show up — with grace, boundaries, and peace.

And trust: if someone leaves your life because of your faith…

Allah will replace them with someone better for your soul.

Not always right away.

But in time. And with wisdom.

My Experience With Relatives and Friends Changing

When I took shahada, some of my relatives and closest friends seemed supportive at first, but then I noticed the distance. Invitations stopped, conversations felt filtered, and I wasn't included in group chats anymore. I gave my aunt an English version of the Quran and she just ignored it.

One friend even told me, "I miss the old you."

And I remember thinking, I miss parts of her too… but this version of me has peace.

I didn't blame them. But I let go.

And slowly, Allah sent new friends.

People who didn't just tolerate my faith — they shared it.

And being able to say "In sha' Allah" without explaining it? That felt like coming home.

You Can Still Love Them — From a Distance

You don't have to burn bridges to protect your peace.

You can love someone and know your values no longer align.

You can pray for someone even if they never ask about your faith.

You can wish them well while making space for new relationships that reflect your growth.

This doesn't make you fake or fickle.

It makes you faithful — to who you are becoming.

The Prophet Muhammad ﷺ Faced This Too

Even the Prophet Muhammad ﷺ lost people when he embraced the truth.

His uncles. His childhood friends. His neighbors.

He was mocked, boycotted, hurt by those who once knew and loved him.

But he never responded with hate.

He never gave up hope.

He continued his mission with mercy, knowing that he was not alone.

And neither are you.

How to Move Forward With Grace

Give people a chance to adjust.

Sometimes it takes time for them to see this version of you.

Set boundaries when needed.

You don't have to attend events or conversations that compromise your faith.

Leave the door open — if it's safe.

A kind message. A check-in. A smile. Sometimes hearts soften later.

Make du'a for them.

Not out of pity — but out of love. They once held a part of your heart.

Seek your people.

Ask Allah to send you those who love you for who you are —
and remind you of who you're becoming.

A New Kind of Friendship Awaits

You will find sisters and brothers in faith who feel like family.

You will laugh, connect, and feel seen again — without
compromise.

These friendships may start slowly.

But they will root deeply.

And when you say "for the sake of Allah," you'll understand what
true companionship feels like.

Heart Reflection: A Du'a for This Chapter

Ya Allah…

Heal the ache I feel from friendships I've outgrown.

Give me the courage to let go when I need to.

And the wisdom to love people without losing myself.

Surround me with those who draw me closer to You.

Let me be a friend who uplifts, reflects, and protects faith.

And if I ever feel alone — remind me that You are enough.

Ameen.

Heart Journal 24

Write about a friendship that changed after you embraced Islam. How did it make you feel?

What would you say to that friend if you could speak from the heart?

What qualities do you now seek in your closest companions?

Heart Journal 24

Heart Journal 24

CHAPTER 25

CARRYING ISLAM INTO YOUR FAMILY LIFE

You didn't grow up praying five times a day.

You didn't grow up fasting in Ramadan. You didn't hear the adhan in your childhood home. You didn't have parents or cousins reminding you to say *Bismillah* before eating.

So now, after embracing Islam, your home feels like a new world… built from scratch. And sometimes, it's beautiful. Other times — it's lonely.

Because even though your heart has changed, not everyone in your family understands.

When You're the Only Muslim in the Family

You might feel like the odd one out at dinners, parties, holidays. You might get asked questions you're too tired to answer. You might feel judged, even unintentionally. Or you might feel deeply loved — but never quite understood.

And that's okay. You don't have to be fully understood to be fully sincere. Even if no one else in your household practices Islam… your sincerity still lights up the space.

Small Acts, Big Ripples

You don't have to preach. You don't have to debate. You don't have to explain every decision.

Sometimes, *da'wah* looks like: — Kindness when it's hard — Patience when no one notices — Quiet prayers in your room — Smiling when you refuse something you used to accept — Gently setting new boundaries, again and again

Every moment of integrity in front of your family is a seed planted — even if it takes years to grow.

Navigating the Questions

"Why can't you eat this anymore?" "Just skip praying this once." "Are you still doing that fasting thing?" "You used to be fun." "You're not like *those* Muslims, right?" "So… when are you going back to normal?"

These words can sting, even when said with a smile. And it's okay to feel tired. It's okay to not always have the perfect answer.

You're not responsible for changing hearts — only for protecting your own. Respond with calm. Or silence. Or walk away when needed. Boundaries are allowed. And your peace matters.

What If My Family Never Accepts It?

That's one of the hardest parts of this journey. Some families never come around. Some tolerate but never embrace. Some fight your faith until the end.

But Allah sees your restraint. He sees the du'as you make behind closed doors. He sees the love you hold — even when you're misunderstood.

And He is the One who can soften any heart. Even if it takes years. Even if it doesn't happen in your lifetime.

When No One Applauds — Allah Rewards

There will be no likes. No retweets. No applause.

Just the smile of your own soul… and the pleasure of your Lord. And on the Day of Judgment, when deeds are weighed, you may find that the ones done in silence tip the scale the most.

A Legacy of Quiet Goodness

And maybe… maybe that quiet da'wah you're doing today was planted long before your shahada. Maybe the values of compassion, giving, and integrity were already in your bones — just waiting to be reawakened through Islam.

That's what I realized about my own parents.

My Parents Taught Me What Quiet Goodness Looks Like

Long before I knew what *ibadah* meant, my parents were showing me what it looked like to serve quietly — and with heart.

My father rarely celebrated his birthday the way most people do. Instead, he would spend that day sponsoring spiritual retreats for men — sometimes traveling far from home, giving lectures, and dedicating his time to helping others reconnect with God.

Even as a child, I noticed his absence on those days. But now I see: His sacrifice wasn't just about giving money — he gave himself.

He also generously gave to help rebuild the church in our village. Not for praise or position, but because he believed in caring for the spiritual needs of the community. It wasn't flashy. It wasn't announced. But it mattered — and it shaped the way I later understood *sadaqah*.

My mother, too, had a heart that saw without being asked. She became the quiet refuge of our neighbors during hardship.

People would come to her privately, in need — and she would give without hesitation. There was no shame, no judgment. Just a woman who had little, but gave much.

At the time, I didn't understand how those moments would live in me. But now, as I reflect on the beauty of private acts of worship — giving quietly, praying unseen, showing up when no one is clapping — I see where it began.

Even before Islam, Allah was shaping my heart to love sincerity.

The Hope Hidden in Everyday Moments

When your parent says, "I'm proud of you," even if they don't understand... When your child repeats *Alhamdulillah* because they hear it from you... When your home smells of suhoor or echoes with du'a... When your presence makes others ask questions — not to challenge, but to learn...

These are wins. Small. Sacred. Soul-shaping wins.

Be Patient With Yourself Too

You're learning how to carry Islam while holding onto your family ties. That's no small thing.

Give yourself grace if you feel emotionally torn. You can love your family and still say no to things. You can be firm in faith and gentle in tone. You can show up differently now — and still be their daughter, sibling, parent, friend.

Heart Reflection: A Du'a for This Chapter

Ya Allah… Let me carry Islam into my home with wisdom and love. Let me speak with kindness, even when I feel unheard. Protect my heart when I feel alone. Help me stay firm when I feel pressure to compromise. Guide my family toward understanding — in this life or the next. Let them see the light of Islam through my character, not just my words. And if they never fully accept it… let me never doubt that You do.

Ameen.

Heart Journal 25

What has been your biggest challenge in practicing Islam around your family? What does it look like for you to stand in your faith with gentleness? Write a du'a for your family — even the ones who may never say it back.

Heart Journal 25

Heart Journal 25

CHAPTER 26

WHEN YOU MISS SOMEONE WHO ISN'T MUSLIM

There's a particular ache that comes with missing someone you love —

when you know they don't share your faith.

You might still laugh together.

You might still love each other deeply.

You might have history, memories, inside jokes that no one else knows.

But under the surface, there's a quiet ache.

A feeling of:

"We're close in this life… but will we be close in the next?"

It's a grief that's hard to explain — because the person is still here.

But the distance is real. And it lives in your heart.

Not Everyone Understands This Kind of Longing

People may tell you to focus on the Hereafter.

To "just make du'a."

To accept that guidance is in Allah's hands.

And all of that is true.

But it doesn't erase the ache.

Because love doesn't shut off when someone believes differently.

If anything, faith makes you love more deeply —

because now you're not just thinking about time… you're thinking about eternity.

When You See What They Don't See

You wish they could feel the peace you feel in sujood.

You wish they knew the sweetness of saying Bismillah before eating.

You wish they understood why you walk away from certain things, not out of arrogance — but out of love for your Creator.

And when they don't see it —

when they shrug, or tease, or avoid the conversation —

you feel that quiet ache again.

"I want this for you. I want Jannah with you."

That's not judgment. That's love.

The kind that transcends lifestyle, politics, and opinions.

The kind that aches for someone's soul.

You Can Love Without Compromising

It's possible to:

Set boundaries

Protect your values

Stay firm in your faith

and still love someone who isn't Muslim.

That might be a parent.

A best friend.

A sibling.

A child.

A spouse (if you reverted after marriage).

Or even someone you once thought you'd spend your life with.

Islam doesn't demand coldness.

It calls you to mercy, to care, to authenticity.

You don't have to stop loving them.

But you do have to love Allah more.

A Love That Changes

Sometimes, you'll notice that your love evolves.

You become more reserved in conversation.

You avoid certain topics.

You stop sharing every detail of your spiritual growth.

You smile more gently, speak more cautiously, and cry more privately.

And that's okay.

It doesn't mean you love them less.

It means a new priority is refining your love — your relationship with Allah.

That's not distance. That's growth.

Making Du'a With Both Hope and Humility

You may ask Allah:

"Let them see what I see."

"Open their heart the way You opened mine."

"Let me be a reason they're guided."

"Let us be together in Jannah."

And you may ask that du'a with tears, over and over again.

Sometimes, you'll feel hopeful.

Sometimes you'll feel helpless.

Sometimes you'll wonder, "Is this even working?"

But know this: every sincere du'a for someone else is rewarded — whether you see the result or not.

And no du'a made with love is ever wasted.

Holding Space for What's Out of Your Hands

You are not their savior.

You are not their judge.

You are not their guarantee.

You are a witness.

A vessel of kindness.

A reminder, a prayer, a possibility.

And that's enough.

Trust Allah to do the part you can't.

Ask for softening. Ask for signs.

Ask to be part of their guidance — without forcing, without fear.

Because in the end… only He guides hearts.

Love in the Dunya, Hope for the Akhirah

We don't know whose ending will be beautiful.

We don't know how someone's journey will unfold.

So be the kind of Muslim whose presence keeps the door to Islam open.

Whose character is the reason someone reconsiders.

Whose love lingers long after the conversations stop.

And maybe — just maybe — your quiet, consistent, sincere love will be part of their return to their Creator.

Heart Reflection: A Du'a for This Chapter

Ya Allah…

I miss them. And I love them. And I don't know what their future holds.

But You do.

If there's any goodness in me, let it be a light for them.

If there's any moment they soften, let it lead them to You.

Guide them gently. Show them truth wrapped in mercy.

And if I never see it in this life —

let me meet them again in a place where no hearts are heavy.

Let me love them without losing myself.

And let me trust that You are the Most Just, the Most Kind.

Ameen.

Heart Journal 26

Who do you miss that doesn't share your faith? Write a du'a for them from your heart.

What boundaries have helped you stay close without compromising your deen?

What would it mean to fully trust Allah with someone you love — even if the outcome is still unseen?

Heart Journal 26

Heart Journal 26

CHAPTER 27

WHEN ALLAH USES YOU TO GUIDE SOMEONE ELSE

You don't always know when it's happening.

You're just living your life…

trying to be consistent in your prayers,

keeping your heart close to Allah,

staying sincere in your intention.

And then, suddenly —

someone tells you,

"You're the reason I started learning about Islam."

Or asks,

"Why do you do that?"

"Can you teach me to pray?"

"What made you choose this path?"

And you realize:

Allah used you — with all your imperfections — to be part of someone's return to Him.

It humbles you. It amazes you. It makes you want to fall into sujood in awe.

You Never Know Who's Watching

You may not be the loudest da'wah voice.

You may not feel qualified.

You may just be trying to survive your own spiritual journey.

But someone sees your peace and wonders about its source.

Someone sees your discipline and admires your purpose.

Someone sees your patience in a storm — and begins to question what anchors you.

And Allah, in His wisdom, lets your living da'wah reach someone's heart — without a single lecture.

The Most Powerful Da'wah Is How You Live

How you treat your family

How you react under stress

How you walk with humility

How you forgive

How you smile when you say Salam

How you stay calm when misunderstood

These small, ordinary moments often speak louder than any book or debate.

Because people may forget what you said —

but they won't forget how you made them feel.

You Don't Have to Force It

Sometimes we feel pressure to convert people, to convince them.

But your job isn't to guide — it's to invite.

To show up.

To be gentle.

To trust the timing of the One who guides hearts.

The Prophet Muhammad ﷺ couldn't guide even his beloved uncle.

And yet — Allah honored him with guiding nations.

You never know which seed you're planting.

You never know who will take their shahada long after you've parted ways.

But Allah knows. And He writes it all.

The Ripple Effect

Sometimes, your presence leads one person to Islam…

and through them, their children are raised in faith…

and their grandchildren memorize Qur'an…

and sadaqah flows for generations.

You may never see it in your lifetime —

but your reward continues long after you're gone.

That's the power of being used for good.

When It Happens, Give Credit Where It's Due

It's easy to feel proud when someone says you inspired them.

And yes — it's a beautiful thing to be appreciated.

But always redirect the glory:

"All praise is for Allah. I'm still learning, too."

"It's really Allah who guided us both."

Because when you stay humble, Allah increases your impact.

And when you stay grateful, He increases your reward.

Even a Single Moment Can Matter

Maybe it's the one time you wore hijab confidently.

Maybe it's the kindness you showed someone in the drive-thru.

Maybe it's your quiet remembrance in a shared space.

The moment may be brief.

But its echo can last forever.

Don't underestimate the weight of your worship.

Someone's life may change just by watching you live yours with sincerity.

Heart Reflection: A Du'a for This Chapter

Ya Allah…

If You ever choose to use me as a means of someone's guidance

let me receive it with humility.

Let me never forget that You are the One who guides hearts.

Let me live in a way that reflects the beauty of Islam,

even in silence.

Make my worship a light that reaches others.

Make my presence a reminder of Your mercy.

And if anyone finds You through me —

let me find closeness to You through them, too.

Ameen.

Heart Journal 27

Have you ever witnessed someone take shahada? What did it stir in your heart?

Reflect on a time someone said you inspired them in their faith. How did that moment shape you?

What does it mean to you to be a living example of Islam — and how can you carry that responsibility with humility?

Heart Journal 27

Heart Journal 27

CHAPTER 28

THE QUIET POWER OF FORGIVENESS

The Sunnah You Fell in Love With

There are many beautiful Sunnahs to fall in love with — smiling at a stranger, fasting Mondays & Thursdays and the middle of the month, praying tahajjud, giving in secret, making du'a for someone behind their back, greeting with peace. But the one that changed me the most was the Sunnah of forgiveness.

Not the kind of forgiveness you offer when someone is remorseful and asks for it. But the kind you offer when no apology ever comes. When your name has been damaged. When others look at you differently because of something untrue they heard. And yet — you choose to let go. Quietly. For the sake of Allah.

There was a sister once who tried to ruin my reputation. Not by twisting my words, but by planting doubts in the hearts of others. I learned about what she was doing. I could see it unfolding. It was painful. And it wasn't random. It was driven by jealousy. By competition I never asked for.

She never came to me. Never admitted anything. Never asked for forgiveness.

But I gave it anyway.

Because I realized I didn't want her to occupy that much space in my mind. I didn't want her actions to echo through my thoughts while I was trying to recite Qur'an, or enjoy a peaceful meal, or fall asleep at night. She had already taken enough — I wouldn't let her take my inner stillness too.

So I forgave. Not loudly. Not publicly. But inwardly — as a form of worship.

Not because I'm perfect or unaffected. But because I remembered the Prophet Muhammad ﷺ — the one who forgave those who harmed him, who slandered him, who threw stones at him until his blessed feet bled. He forgave not because they deserved it — but because he loved Allah more than his ego.

"Let them pardon and overlook. Would you not love for Allah to forgive you?" — Surah An-Nur (24:22)

And so I let go.

I didn't make an announcement. I didn't seek revenge. I just moved on — with less weight in my heart. I prayed for her quietly. Not because she earned it. But because I needed it. Because I didn't want her actions to harden me or make me bitter.

Forgiveness, I've come to realize, is not weakness. It's strength. It's prophetic. It's Sunnah.

And it's one of the most beautiful things I've ever learned to do.

Heart Reflection: Letting Go for the Sake of Allah

Forgiveness doesn't always come with closure. Sometimes, you forgive without the full story. Without an apology. Without justice in this world. But you forgive anyway — because you trust that Allah knows, sees, and will restore what was broken.

You forgive because your heart is not a home for bitterness. Because you want to stand before Allah with a heart that's soft — not swollen with pain or pride. You forgive because your role model ﷺ taught you how.

And sometimes… forgiving is how you free yourself.

Du'a: *O Allah, soften my heart with the light of Your mercy. Protect me from resentment that clouds my soul. Help me to forgive those who never asked, And raise me in the ranks of those You love — the ones who choose mercy over revenge, silence over slander, and grace over grudges. Ameen.*

Heart Journal 28

Is there someone I've been holding in my heart with quiet anger or unspoken pain?

What would it feel like to let it go — not for them, but for Allah?

Write a private du'a or a letter you'll never send. Let the words release the weight. Let it be your own act of prophetic mercy.

Heart Journal 28

Heart Journal 28

CHAPTER 29

THE ONES WHO WALKED BESIDE ME

Islam is a journey, but it's never meant to be walked alone. Along the way, Allah places people in your life who don't just witness your transformation — they nurture it. They remind you to pray when your heart feels distant. They laugh with you when the world feels heavy. They hold your hand when you feel like disappearing.

For me, those people have names:

Sisters Damaliya. Lita. Zayna.

These women have been more than friends.

They've been anchors. Compasses. Reminders of who I am and who I want to be.

Sister Damaliya is strong, wise, and full of soul. She has always had a way of speaking reminders with gentle firmness. She nudges me to memorize more Qur'an, observe the sunnah fasts, and push a little further toward Allah for extra rewards. She guided and picked me up when I was in my lowest moments. She cares more about the akhirah than the dunya. And somehow, she does all this while also preparing the most nourishing meals she lovingly serves us with care. She reminds me that discipline can be wrapped in warmth. And beyond all that — she prays. I will never forget how she made heartfelt du'a for both me and Zayna to have righteous, loving, iman-filled husbands. And Allah, in His mercy, answered. What a gift it is to be loved by someone who calls upon your name in the unseen.

Sister Lita — the quiet warrior. She carries joy in her spirit like a lantern, but behind her smile is a well of resilience. I've watched her face hardships that would shake most people — and yet, she endures them with patience and grace. What humbles me most is that she never lets her small disability hold her back. She works hard. She shows up. She contributes with both strength and sincerity. Even on the hard days, she finds a way to carry on — not just surviving, but shining. Her faith glows through her trials. Lita reminds me that joy is not the absence of pain — it's the presence of **sabr**. And that strength doesn't always raise its voice. Sometimes, it just quietly refuses to give up.

Sister Zayna — my quirky, beautiful burst of light.

With her, even the simple things turn into joy. Whether it's the excitement of buying new hijabs, Islamic books, or a new color-coded Quran or our shared laughter during late-night talks after AlMaghrib seminars, she brings lightness into the faith journey. We've ridden Metra trains to learn more 'ilm, shared snacks, notes, and reflections—and in those moments, I realized how beautiful it is to grow in Islam *together*.

These women weren't just companions.

They were soul sisters.

They met me where I was and helped me walk further.

In a world where reverts often feel alone, Allah gifted me a circle I didn't know I needed.

Was it Qadr that we have all met?

Women who loved me through my growth.

Who held my story with gentleness.

Who never rushed my process but never let me settle either.

As reverts, we often carry the weight of trying to "get it right." But sometimes, part of getting it right… is learning to laugh again. To gather. To rejoice. To dance around the kitchen while making salad or samosas. To asking for recipes and ingredients of what sister Damaliya put in her delicious Biryani. I wasn't at a masjid. I wasn't dressed fancy. But I was surrounded by people who understood me. We played games, shared food, and laughed until we cried. And I remember thinking, "This is worship too." This togetherness. This halal joy. This feeling of belonging.

Worship isn't always in sujood.

Sometimes it's in your smile.

Sometimes, it's in the way you hug a friend who needs it.

Sometimes it's in allowing yourself to feel happy after so many hard days.

Joy, when done in remembrance of Allah — is not a distraction.

It's a reflection of gratitude.

And gratitude is worship.

To you, sisters Damaliya, Lita, and Zayna, I pray Allah gathers us together again—not just in this life but in Jannah.

Heart Reflection: When Friendship Feels Like Du'a Answered

True companionship in Islam is not loud or flashy.

It's a quiet knowing.

A shared glance before prayer.

A sister who says, "Let's memorize this together."

A friend who holds space for your struggle and still makes you laugh.

Some friends are du'as in disguise.

And Allah knows just when to send them.

Du'a for My Sisters in Faith *O Allah, Most Loving, Most Generous— Bless these women who have walked beside me in this journey of faith. Reward Sister Damaliya for every quiet reminder, every prayer she whispered for me in secret, and every meal served with love. Strengthen Sister Lita, whose patience and resilience shine in ways the world may never see—grant her ease, healing, and joy that never fades. And bless Sister Zayna, the burst of light You placed in my life. Keep her laughter bright, her faith firm, and bless her children with strong iman and heart always near to Yours.*

Record their kindness in books of light. Protect them, elevate them, and never let them feel unseen..

Ya Allah, preserve our sisterhood in this life and reunite us in the next—under Your Shade, near Your Throne, in the company of the Prophet Muhammad ﷺ.

Ameen

Heart Journal 29

Reflect and write:

Who are the people who helped you stay rooted in your faith journey?

What specific moments or traits from their friendship impacted you most?

How has Allah used your sisters in Islam to remind you of His mercy and love?

Complete this du'a:

"Ya Allah, bless the ones who loved me through my becoming. Grant them..."

Heart Journal 29

Heart Journal 29

CHAPTER 30

PLANTING SEEDS YOU'LL NEVER SEE BLOOM

Some of the most meaningful things you will do for Allah…
you may never witness the result.

The kind word that stopped someone from walking away from
Islam. The book you gifted that stayed unopened for years —
until the day they were ready. The du'a you made for a stranger
who never even knew your name.

We often crave certainty. We want to *see* the fruit. But Allah
teaches us that reward is not always in the outcome — it's in the
intention, the sincerity, and the quiet surrender of trusting that
He sees what we don't.

Some seeds don't sprout in front of you. Some bloom long after
you've gone. And some — Allah allows to grow in hearts you'll
never meet, in generations you'll never live to see.

If you ever feel like your efforts are small, unnoticed, or slow…
remember Nuh, peace be upon him preached for 950 years, and
still, only a few followed. The weight of truth is never measured
by numbers — but by the purity with which it's carried.

You don't need to be loud to leave a legacy. You just need to be
sincere. Keep planting. Keep praying. Even if you never see the
garden.

Not every act of da'wah looks like a lecture. Not every invitation to Islam is loud. Sometimes, the most powerful form of uplift is simply being yourself — fully, quietly, faithfully.

In a beautiful way.

Because what I thought was a weakness — was actually a connection.

What I thought made me less of a Muslim — was what made someone else feel less alone.

Every revert becomes, in time, a bridge.

Between fear and faith.

Between loneliness and belonging.

Just be real. Be kind. Be available.

Sometimes, uplifting others is as simple as replying to a message. Smiling when you see a new face at the masjid.

Or writing a book like this — not because you have all the answers, but because you remember what it felt like to have none.

A Du'a for the Seeds We May Never See

Ya Allah, Let the quiet things I do for Your sake become light on the Day I meet You. Let my words, my prayers, my sacrifices — even the ones no one remembers — be written with mercy on my record.

If I inspire someone, let it be because You placed barakah in my actions. If I help someone return to You, let it be from Your will, not my worth.

Ya Rabb, Accept from me what is broken, what is unseen, what is trembling but sincere. And make my life a path of goodness — even if I never see where it leads.

Ameen.

Heart Journal 30

What "seeds" have you planted in your life — small acts of goodness, da'wah, or advice — that you may never see the outcome of?

Write about the things you did quietly, sincerely, maybe even in pain or uncertainty… but you did them for Allah. What do you hope blooms from them, even if not in your lifetime?

And what seeds are you being called to plant now — even if no one claps for you, even if no one ever knows?

Heart Journal 30

Heart Journal 30

PART V

TRUSTING THE JOURNEY- TAWAKKUL, GRATITUDE, AND HOPE

CHAPTER 31

HOW GRATITUDE SOFTENS THE HARD DAYS

There are days when everything feels heavy.

The dishes pile up.

The house is a mess.

The prayers feel rushed.

The world feels chaotic, and your heart feels slow to respond.

You're tired, irritable, and wondering if your efforts even matter.

And then — in the middle of the noise — you pause.

And whisper: "Alhamdulillah."

Not because everything is perfect.

But because, somehow, even in the struggle... You still have enough to say thank you.

Gratitude Isn't Just for Good Days

Gratitude in Islam isn't reserved for mountaintop moments.

It's a way of seeing — a shift in heart posture, even in difficulty.

Allah reminds us again and again:

"If you are grateful, I will surely increase you."

(Surah Ibrahim 14:7)

Gratitude doesn't erase your problems.

It doesn't silence pain.

But it makes the hard days softer.

The burdens lighter.

The silence is more meaningful.

Bismillah in Everyday Moments

There was a season when my heart felt scattered.

I wasn't doing anything "big" in worship — no long nights of prayer, no intensive Qur'an study.

Just simple, ordinary days.

But I began something new:

Saying Bismillah before every little task.

Before entering a room.

Before cutting fruit.

Before stirring a pot.

Before turning the key in the door.

And that small act — that one word — became my grounding.

It was as if I was inviting Allah into the ordinary.

And over time, those little Bismillah moments became threads of peace woven through my day.

What We Often Overlook

We tend to think of gratitude as something grand:

Writing long journal entries

Giving big speeches of thanks

Feeling deeply emotional

But sometimes, gratitude is quiet.

It looks like:

Breathing deeply and whispering Alhamdulillah

Pausing to notice the taste of warm food

Feeling the softness of your prayer rug under your forehead

Seeing the blue sky and remembering the One who made it

Drinking cold water and knowing it could have been otherwise

The Prophet Muhammad ﷺ said:

"Whoever among you wakes up secure in his property, healthy in his body, and has his food for the day, it is as if the world has been gathered for him."

(Tirmidhi)

Sometimes, Jannah feels far.

But small thank-you's bring it closer.

Gratitude Even When It's Hard

It might feel unnatural to say "Alhamdulillah" when:

You're sick

You're grieving

You've lost a job

You're doubting yourself

But that's when it becomes even more powerful.

Not forced. Not fake.

But a whisper from the soul:

"Ya Allah, even now… I trust that You're still giving me what I need."

That kind of gratitude transforms your heart.

It doesn't ignore pain — it invites Allah into it.

How to Build a Gentle Habit of Gratitude

Pick a daily anchor.

After Fajr, pause to list three blessings.

Say Alhamdulillah aloud.

Let your tongue train your heart.

Start a **"Gratitude for the Tiny Things"** list.

The smell of rain. The warmth of tea. The voice of a loved one.

Make du'a in gratitude.

Instead of asking, spend a few minutes just thanking Allah.

Connect every praise back to the Source.

Not just "I love this view" — but "Ya Allah, thank You for letting me see this today."

Gratitude Is a Gateway

When you say thank You often, it becomes easier to:

Accept what you can't control

Trust Allah's timing

Find joy in imperfection

See tests as invitations, not punishments

Gratitude opens your heart.

And when your heart is open — it's softer, stronger, and more able to receive love from your Creator.

Your Thankfulness Is Worship

It doesn't have to be fancy.

It doesn't have to be posted.

It doesn't even have to be understood by others.

Gratitude, when done for Allah's sake, is ibadah.

Even a whispered "Ya Allah, thank You for this breath" is written in your book of good deeds.

So never underestimate the power of noticing — and praising — the ordinary.

Because the ordinary, when seen through the eyes of iman, becomes extraordinary.

Heart Reflection: A Du'a for This Chapter

Ya Allah…

Let me notice the blessings I usually miss.

Let my tongue be soft with gratitude.

Let my eyes see Your mercy in the details of my day.

When I feel overwhelmed, remind me to pause and say Alhamdulillah.

When I feel numb, remind me of how much You've already given.

Let gratitude soften my impatience, quiet my worries, and deepen my trust.

Let it be my worship — and my healing.

Ameen.

Heart Journal 31

What are five small things you're grateful for today — things you usually overlook?

How can saying Bismillah or Alhamdulillah throughout your day help you feel closer to Allah?

Write about a time when gratitude helped you get through something hard.

Heart Journal 31

Heart Journal 31

CHAPTER 32

EMBRACING YOUR UNIQUE JOURNEY WITHOUT COMPARISON

You see her quoting Qur'an with ease.

You hear him reciting surahs from memory.

You notice the way they pray, fast, study, serve — all with apparent serenity.

And a voice inside you whispers:

"You're behind."

"You should be doing more."

"Why don't you have that kind of faith yet?"

Even in the most sacred spaces, comparison can sneak in.

Quietly. Subtly.

Turning moments of inspiration into moments of self-doubt.

The Danger of Spiritual Comparison

It's good to be inspired.

But comparison is a thief — not just of joy, but of sincerity.

Because when you measure your progress against someone else's pace,

you forget that Allah didn't create your path to match theirs.

You're not here to copy anyone else's Islam.

You're here to build a relationship with Allah that's yours — intimate, raw, and real.

Everyone Starts Somewhere Different

Some people grew up in Muslim households.

Some learned Arabic as toddlers.

Some had parents who woke them up for Fajr and taught them du'as before bed.

Others found Islam in adulthood.

Or after trauma.

Or through a slow awakening that took years.

And some are still figuring out how to believe while healing from the past.

That's the beauty of this ummah — it holds all kinds of souls on all kinds of timelines.

The Pressure to "Catch Up"

As a revert, you might feel like you're constantly playing spiritual catch-up.

You want to memorize more.

Learn faster.

Pray "properly."

Be fluent in du'a.

Understand everything — yesterday.

And when you don't meet that standard, you might feel unworthy. Ashamed.

Like you're falling behind in a race you never agreed to run.

But here's the truth:

Allah does not grade you on speed. He sees your effort. He sees your heart.

And that's what counts.

A Time I Compared — and Crumbled

There was a time I saw other sisters doing so much more than I was.

They were memorizing surahs, attending halaqahs, even traveling to study Islam abroad.

And I felt small. Embarrassed. Like my little daily efforts — a whispered du'a here, a late-night prayer there — were somehow less than theirs.

It made me rush.

Overcommit.

Say yes to everything.

Try to prove I was a "real" Muslim.

But all it did was leave me exhausted. Spiritually numb.

That's when I realized that competitiveness in faith, when rooted in insecurity, is not noble—it's draining.

And Allah didn't ask me to be someone else.

He asked me to be sincere — in my lane, with my tools, in my season.

Faith Isn't a Performance

It's not a checklist.

It's not a show.

It's not a ladder where some sit higher than others.

Faith is a relationship.

And relationships take time.

They grow with honesty.

They deepen through consistency, not comparison.

If the only prayer you can make today is tired and distracted — it still counts.

If all you can offer is a short dhikr while doing dishes — it still counts.

If your iman feels soft, shaky, slow — it still counts.

Because Allah sees sincerity in what others might overlook.

Walk at Your Pace — and Don't Apologize for It

Maybe you're learning to read Qur'an at 35.

Maybe you're wearing hijab slowly, step by step.

Maybe you've missed more Ramadans than you've kept.

Maybe you've taken three steps forward and two steps back.

That doesn't make your journey invalid.

Your path might not be linear — but it's yours.

And Allah never belittles the small, imperfect steps taken in love for Him.

What Matters Most

Not how fast you reach a goal —

but how sincere your effort was.

Not how fluent your Arabic is —

but how present your heart was when you said Ya Allah.

Not how much you know —

but how much you live what you know.

And above all:

That you keep returning, again and again, even when you fall short.

Heart Reflection: A Du'a for This Chapter

Ya Allah…

Let me love the path You've written for me.

Let me walk it with peace, not pressure.

Protect me from comparing my pace to others.

Remind me that You see my struggles, my tears, my growth — even when no one else does.

Let me be inspired without feeling inferior.

Let me admire without self-doubt.

And let my journey be beautiful — not because it's perfect, but because it's sincere.

Ameen.

Heart Journal 32

What parts of your faith journey have felt "behind," "different," or "not enough" when you compared yourself to others?

Write about a moment when you felt like everyone else was doing more — learning faster, memorizing more, praying better.

Heart Journal 32

Heart Journal 32

CHAPTER 33

WHEN YOU TRUST THE QUIET PLAN

Not all guidance is loud.

Sometimes Allah's plan doesn't arrive with lightning bolts or sudden clarity. Sometimes, it's a quiet unfolding — like a flower that blooms before you even realize the season has changed.

You may not understand why one door closed. Why that relationship ended. Why that opportunity slipped away. But in the quiet, there is still a plan.

And trusting that plan means learning to hold peace even when the road ahead feels invisible.

It means praying, even when you don't feel the answer. It means taking the next small step, even when you can't see the whole staircase. It means believing that Allah is never late, never forgetful, and never absent — even when your heart feels unanswered.

There will be seasons in your life when it seems like nothing is happening. But beneath the surface, roots are growing. You are being prepared. Protected. Positioned.

You don't need to know the whole story yet. You just need to trust the One who's writing it.

Because one day — maybe not today, maybe not tomorrow — you will look back and whisper, *"That moment of silence was a mercy." "That delay was a doorway." "That unanswered du'a was a better redirection."*

And you'll realize…

You were never lost. You were being led.

Some of the best things in my life began with a *"No."*

Or a silence I didn't understand.

Or a heartbreak I didn't think I could recover from.

There's something deeply humbling about trusting Allah's plan when you can't see where it's leading. When the doors close. When the people leave. When the du'a goes unanswered — or so you think.

But time passes.

And suddenly, what once felt like a wound becomes a window.

A redirection. A protection.

A quiet mercy.

I've had moments in my life when I begged Allah for something I thought would bring me happiness—a relationship, an opportunity, a path I believed was right. And when it didn't come, I felt confused, unseen, forgotten.

But later — sometimes years later — I would whisper, *"Alhamdulillah, it didn't happen."*

Because what He gave instead was better.

Maybe not easier. But better for my heart. Better for my growth.

Better for my akhirah.

Allah is not a careless Author.

He writes every line of your story with knowledge, mercy, and love.

You may not understand the chapter you're living right now.

But one day, it will make sense.

And until then, trust the quiet plan.

Heart Reflection: When You Didn't Get What You Prayed For

Sometimes Allah doesn't give you what you asked for…

Because He's protecting you from something you can't yet see.

Because He's preparing you for something greater.

Because He wants your heart to stay with Him — not be distracted by the thing you thought would save you.

The waiting isn't punishment.

The silence isn't neglect.

It's refinement. Redirection.

Love — in a form that doesn't always look the way you imagined.

A Du'a for Trusting the Quiet Plan

Ya Allah, When I cannot see the path ahead, let me still walk with You. When things don't go the way I hoped, let me not fall into despair. Replace the noise of my doubt with the calm of Your wisdom. Soften my heart to accept that delay is not denial — it is divine design.

Let me trust the doors You open… and trust even more the ones You gently close. Let my waiting be worship. Let my silence be surrender. And let my story unfold in the rhythm You have written, not the one I imagined.

You are Al-Latīf — the Subtle, the Gentle. And I trust that even what I do not understand is already a mercy in motion.

Ameen.

Heart Journal: His Plan > My Plan

Think of a time when something didn't work out — but later, you saw its wisdom. What was that moment?

Complete this du'a in your own words:

"Ya Allah, even when I don't understand… I trust You because…"

Heart Journal 33

CHAPTER 34

WHEN ALLAH WRITES A NEW LOVE STORY

There's a kind of heartbreak that feels final.

Divorce.

Abandonment.

A family member you deeply care about neglecting you.

A love you thought would last… ending.

As a revert, you might carry the added weight of wondering:

"Will anyone understand my story now?"

"Who would want someone with a past?"

"Is love — halal, healing love — still possible for someone like me?"

The world may tell you it's over.

That you've missed your chance.

That your "ideal" is behind you.

But Allah writes stories no one sees coming.

And sometimes, your real beginning comes after the ending you never wanted.

Grieving the First Chapter

After a painful separation, you may go through every emotion:

Regret

Guilt

Shame

Anger

Neglect

Fear of the future

Grief over what could've been

You might replay the memories.

Blame yourself.

Blame them.

Ask Allah why. Cry over your du'as, which seemed to go unanswered.

And still, Allah is there — listening, softening, preparing.

Because your story didn't end.

It's being rewritten.

And suddenly, all the pain that had once crushed me became part of the path that led to this blessing.

If that chapter in my life hadn't happened,

I wouldn't have met a better man.

Or found a better life.

Or become a better version of me.

Allah Isn't Done With You

You may feel like the past defines you.

That the scars mark you.

That no one will see beyond what you've lost.

But Allah sees what you're becoming.

And when He removes something — even something you begged for —

it's because what He wants to give you is better for your soul.

Not just your desires. Not just your heart.

Your soul.

Love Doesn't Always Arrive on Time — It Arrives on Allah's Time

It may not happen when you expect.

It may not look like your original plan.

It may come in a form you never imagined.

But when it's written for you —

it will come with sakinah (tranquility).

No begging.

No chasing.

No pretending.

Just a peace that feels like prayer answered — not because it's perfect, but because it's right.

When You're Waiting, Not Withering

It's okay to want love.

To ask for it in your du'as.

To keep your heart soft — even after it's been broken.

Just don't let the waiting make you bitter.

Let it make you better.

Use this time to:

Strengthen your worship

Heal your wounds

Clarify your values

Rebuild your confidence in the One who never left

Because the more whole you feel with Allah,

the more peaceful any future love will feel.

Red Flags, Green Lights

One of the gifts of past pain is clarity.

Now, you see red flags earlier.

You ask deeper questions.

You prioritize deen over charm.

You move slower — and with more sincerity.

And when something good comes along,

you don't doubt your worthiness of it.

You see it as part of the mercy you've grown into.

A New Love That Reflects Faith

When Allah writes your next love story —

whether through marriage, friendship, or renewed self-love —

it won't just fill your time.

It will elevate your iman.

It will remind you that you're not "too late."

That nothing is wasted.

That healing isn't the end of your story — it's the start of something better.

Heart Reflection: A Du'a for This Chapter

Ya Allah…

If love is written for me, let it be a love that brings me closer to You.

Let it be patient. Pure. Purposeful.

Heal me from the pains of the past.

Remove the doubts I've carried.

And when You send someone into my life,

let them see my soul — not just my scars.

Make me a source of calm for them,

as they are for me.

And let every heartbreak I've lived through

lead me closer to the kind of love You always knew I needed.

Ameen.

Heart Journal 34

Reflect on how your understanding of love has changed since becoming Muslim.

What did you believe about your future after your last heartbreak? How has Allah surprised you?

If you were writing a du'a for a future love — what qualities would you ask Allah to bless it with?

Heart Journal 34

Heart Journal 34

CHAPTER 35

JANNAH IS WORTH EVERYTHING YOU'VE GIVEN UP

You gave up things you once loved.

Habits. Relationships. Places.

Ways of dressing. Speaking. Thinking.

You said no to invitations that used to excite you.

You stayed quiet when mocked.

You walked away when it would've been easier to stay.

You've cried in the dark.

You've sat in loneliness.

You've questioned if it's worth it.

And still, you choose this path — again and again.

Not because it's easy.

But because your heart knows:

You're walking toward Jannah.

Your Sacrifices Are Not Forgotten

It can be easy to forget how much you've changed.

How far you've come.

Because the growth happened in quiet places:

Behind closed doors

In the silence of early Fajr

In moments when no one clapped for you

But Allah never misses a single step.

He sees the temptations you resist.

The old wounds you don't reopen.

The tears you catch before they fall.

And He promises:

"Indeed, the righteous will be in pleasure… Reclining on adorned couches. They will not see therein any [burning] sun or [freezing] cold."

(Surah Al-Insān 76:11–13)

The Struggle Is the Sign

Sometimes you wonder:

"Why is this still hard?"

"Shouldn't I feel strong by now?"

But the very fact that you struggle and still choose obedience —

that's the sign of your sincerity.

Jannah was never promised to the perfect.

It was promised to the persistent.

"Do the people think they will be left to say 'We believe' and they will not be tested?"

(Surah Al-'Ankabūt 29:2)

Your test is proof of your faith.

And your tears are proof that your heart still wants Allah — even when it hurts.

Every "No" for Allah Is a "Yes" to Jannah

You said no to certain gatherings.

No to fitting in.

No to temporary highs.

No to doing what you used to do.

And in that space… you said yes to something far greater:

Yes to self-respect

Yes to purity

Yes to accountability

Yes, to the peace that only Allah can give

You gave up a world that was fading — to build a life that will last forever.

That's not loss.

That's wisdom.

When the Loneliness Hits

There will be moments when you feel like the only one choosing this path.

Everyone around you seems to have it easier — no guilt, no restrictions, no fear of falling short.

And in those moments, you may wonder:

"Am I missing out?"

But remember this:

Jannah is not crowded.

And the path to it… is sometimes lonely.

But it is full of light.

And every sacrifice you make echoes in eternity.

What You Gave Up vs. What You'll Gain

Is there any trade-off more worth it than this?

Jannah Is for People Like You

Don't think you're too flawed.

Too late.

Too weak.

Jannah isn't for those who never struggled.

It's for those who struggled and still chose Allah.

The Prophet Muhammad ﷺ told us:

"Jannah is surrounded by hardships, and Hellfire is surrounded by desires."

(Bukhari & Muslim)

You're walking through hardship with your eyes on the reward.

And one day — in sha Allah — you'll look back and say:

"Every hard choice… was worth it."

What Keeps You Going

You don't need applause.

You don't need instant results.

You just need to keep walking.

One prayer at a time

One sacrifice at a time

One Alhamdulillah at a time

Because every time you choose faith over ease,

Allah prepares a reward you cannot even imagine.

"No soul knows what has been hidden for them of comfort as a reward for what they used to do."

(Surah As-Sajdah 32:17)

Heart Reflection: A Du'a for This Chapter

Ya Allah…

I've given up things for You — even when it hurt.

I've walked away from ease, from approval, from comfort.

Remind me that it's not in vain.

Let me feel the sweetness of faith in this life,

and the fullness of Your mercy in the next.

When I feel tempted to go backward,

anchor my heart in hope for Jannah.

And when I finally meet You,

let me hear: "Well done, My servant. Come home."

Ameen.

Heart Journal 35

What's one thing you've given up for the sake of Allah? How did it feel then — and how do you feel about it now?

What image of Jannah brings peace to your heart? Describe it.

How can you remind yourself, when things feel hard, that your sacrifices are seen and honored?

Heart Journal 35

Heart Journal 35

DU'AS FROM A REVERT'S HEART

Some du'as aren't said out loud.

They're whispered through tears.

Written in notebooks.

Felt in the chest before they ever reach the tongue.

These are the kinds of du'as I've made most often.

Especially as a revert.

Because there were things I didn't know how to ask for.

There were moments I didn't even have the words.

Just a heart full of longing — and the quiet hope that Allah understood anyway.

Over the years, I've made du'as that felt clumsy, incomplete, messy.

But I've also learned something beautiful:

Allah listens to the heart, not just the grammar.

And sometimes, the most powerful prayers are the ones you make when no one else knows you're breaking.

So here they are — a few of the ones I've carried.

Maybe they'll sound like yours.

Maybe they'll remind you to whisper again.

Du'a for When You Feel Alone

Ya Allah,

This path is beautiful, but sometimes it feels so quiet.

Let me feel Your nearness when the silence is loud.

Surround me with people who remind me of You.

And never let me forget that You are enough.

Du'a for When You Miss Your Family

Ya Allah,

My love for them hasn't lessened — it's just changed.

Please help me be gentle in my da'wah.

Soften their hearts. Heal the distance.

And guide them like You guided me.

Du'a for When You Doubt Yourself

Ya Allah,

You chose me.

Even when I question myself, help me trust Your choice.

Let me walk this path with sincerity, not perfection.

Du'a for When You Missed a Prayer

Ya Allah,

I fell short today.

Not because I didn't care — but because I'm still learning.

Pull me back. Help me begin again.

Du'a for When You Feel Behind

Ya Allah,

It looks like everyone else is ahead of me.

Fluent, confident, steady.

Help me stop comparing.

Let me love the pace You chose for me.

Du'a for When You Fall into Sin Again

Ya Allah,

I slipped. Again.

Please don't shut the door.

Wrap me in Your mercy.

Let this regret pull me closer — not push me away.

Du'a for When You Feel Spiritually Numb

Ya Allah,

The fire inside feels small.

I miss feeling close to You.

Reawaken my heart. Let me feel again. Let me care again.

Du'a for When You Feel Like You're Starting Over — Again

Ya Allah, I've fallen more times than I can count. I've taken steps forward and then stepped back again. But You… You never pushed me away. You keep the door open, even when I walk past it. You call me back with gentleness. Remind me that starting over is not failure — it's a return. And You love when I return.

Du'a for When You Feel Different in the Ummah

Ya Rabb, Sometimes I feel like I don't quite fit. Like I'm too new, too different, too late. Let me find belonging in Your eyes — even when I feel unseen in the crowd. Surround me with people who understand my heart, who welcome me without question, and who remind me that I am never alone.

Du'a for Quiet Growth No One Sees

Ya Allah, You see me trying. Even when no one else does. Even when there are no posts, no praise, no perfection. Just me, whispering Your name in the dark, trying to pray better, trying to learn more, trying to be Yours. Let that be enough. Let it be loved. Let it be accepted.

Du'a for When You Begin to Bloom

Ya Allah,

Thank You for the quiet growth.

For the things You healed without me even noticing.

For the strength You placed in my smile.

Let this blooming be a sign that I'm walking toward You.

These are not polished. They're not perfect.

But they're real.

And if they live anywhere —

they live in the heart of someone who once said "Ashhadu" with trembling lips,

and who now walks, falls, rises, and whispers:

"Guide me… again."

Heart Journal 36

A GENTLE WHISPER FORWARD

Final Reflection

To the one still learning how to breathe again after saying La ilaha illa Allah…

You've walked through fear. Through longing. Through grief and hope and joy braided together.

You've prayed, not knowing all the words.

You've stood in rooms where you felt out of place.

You've made mistakes — and you've kept coming back.

And that? That's the essence of blooming.

You are not blooming because you're perfect.

You're blooming because you're still turning to the One who is.

You've learned to say Bismillah when you begin.

You've whispered Astaghfirullah through tears.

You've said Alhamdulillah on both soft and stormy days.

You've grown.

Sometimes slowly.

Sometimes through heartache.

Sometimes in silence.

But still — you've grown.

So, if ever you feel lost again…

if the heaviness returns…

if the road feels quiet or cold or uncertain…

Remember this:

You've been here before — and Allah never left you.

Not when you questioned your place.

Not when you felt like the only one.

Not even when you doubted your own worth.

He was there.

And He still is.

Let this book be a doorway — not the destination.

Keep reading.

Keep listening.

Keep healing.

Keep making room for joy.

Keep remembering that your Islam isn't measured by loudness or fluency or how many people applaud you.

It's measured in your sincerity.

Let's grow and bloom always,

Joyful Hijabi

Glossary of Islamic Terms

Adhān	The Islamic call to prayer, announced from a mosque.
Akhirah	The afterlife; life after death in Islamic belief.
Āyah	A verse of the Qur'an.
Barakah	Blessing or divine grace.
Du'ā'	Personal supplication or prayer to Allah.
Fiqh	Islamic jurisprudence; understanding of Islamic law.
Hadīth	Sayings, actions, and approvals of the Prophet Muhammad ﷺ.
Halāl	Permissible or lawful in Islam.
Harām	Forbidden or impermissible in Islam.
Hijrah	Migration, particularly the Prophet's migration from Makkah to Madinah.
Imān	Faith or belief in Islam.
Istikhārah	A prayer seeking guidance from Allah in decision-making.
Jannah	Paradise; the eternal home of reward in the Hereafter.
Khushū'	Humility and deep presence in prayer.

Qur'ān	The holy book of Islam, believed to be the word of Allah.
Sabr	Patience, endurance, or perseverance.
Salah	The five daily ritual prayers in Islam.
Sawm	Fasting, especially during the month of Ramadan.
Shahādah	The testimony of faith; declaration that there is no god but Allah, and Muhammad ﷺ is His Messenger.
Sujūd	Prostration in prayer, where one places their forehead on the ground.
Tawakkul	Complete trust and reliance on Allah.

9 7 9 8 8 9 3 9 7 6 1 4 4